PUBLISHER'S NOTE

Published by Cole Hart Presents

This is a work of fiction. Names, characters, places, and events are strictly the product of the author or used fictitiously. Any similarities between actual persons, living or dead, events, settings, or locations are entirely coincidental.

Text COLEHART to 22828 to sign up for the mailing list & for new updates for New Releases.

DEDICATION

This series is dedicated in memory of my baby brother, Hassan Turner. I have been reading since I was a teenager, and in the back of my mind I always said I should write a book one day. I never found or made time to write until after I lost my baby brother at the tender age of 23 in a tragic drowning accident July 19, 2015. To make matters worse, my mom had a massive stroke the day before my brother's funeral. I didn't know how to go on but I knew I had to because so many people depend on me. My closest family and friends encouraged me every day to find an outlet and it was then that I finally MADE time to write. I sat down on November 6, 2015, and I have been writing daily since then. Writing has become therapeutic for me as well as kept me sane. It is my hope that you enjoy the ride in this series which I have created for you during my therapy. Keep resting baby brother. I love and miss you dearly!!

ACKNOWLEDGEMENTS

Writing this book has been a dream come true to me. It has been an exciting and satisfying journey all because of God and my awesome support system. I feel so grateful to be able to finally do what I absolutely love. I have far too many people who have encouraged and inspired me to name one by one, but each and every one of you know how much I love and appreciate you. It's more than words can even describe. I hope that each of you enjoy this series as much as I enjoyed writing it. Thanks so much for taking a chance on me. Enjoy and be blessed!!

Prologue

Cameron sped down the highway driving ninety plus miles per hour trying to get away from the lunatic who was chasing behind her. She gripped the steering wheel tight as her heart beat rapidly and tears streamed down her face. She could not believe she had been so stupid and sent those pictures. Not thinking had most definitely backfired on her. One part of her wanted to just let go of the wheel and let her Camaro crash so that this chase would end, however her sane conscience thought about her son Kingston. Not to mention a mental bell went off reminding her about the child she recently found out she was carrying. With that second thought, she quickly cast her impractical thinking aside and regained her composure. The black car behind her was closing in and all she could do was pray. The expectant mother had ignored the beeping noises until her car began to slow down. She then realized she was running out of gas, but the crash that came from behind sent her car flipping violently off of the highway......

Three Years Ago

Chapter 1

It was a hot summer day in June of 2012 and the air seemed dense. Cameron sat in a room filled with women whom she considered to be her closest friends, dreading her upcoming nuptials. She just wasn't ready to jump somebody's broom. Hell, anybody's broom at that. Though as a Christian, it was the highest honor for a woman to be made a wife, Cameron didn't see it that way. She felt as if she were signing her life away to some average ass nigga all because he had a 401K plan. She was in this regrettable position at the favor of her dad, and for that reason alone.

Toya, Sonya, and Shay eyed her closest because they had made several attempts to talk some sense into her before now. They knew her better than any of the other girls, so they figured they would at least make some kind of an impact. *I've come a long way from the girl I use to be,* Cameron thought as she admired herself in the floor length mirror. Some said she could advertise for *World's Finest Chocolate* with her dark silky smooth complexion because she left you with only thoughts of tasting her. Her confidence is what always leaves one to imagine what it would be like to touch, but just staring from a distance would satisfy the imagination because she was just that beautiful.

"Are you sure you wanna go through with this?" Sonya asked. Sonya stood about five feet seven with a honey glow skin tone and light brown eyes. She must have paid her beautician half of her check every week because her weave always looked like it had been blessed by the gods. She didn't always talk much, but when she did she was sincere with her approach.

Cameron rolled her eyes and started thinking about the things she had shared with a few of her girls. *For the last two weeks she had been sick with worry about her upcoming wedding day. She didn't have the happy feeling that brides to be should have. She should have butterflies in her stomach like an eager school girl right? Her conscience yet again failed her. She tried to force herself to be happy about the decision she had made, but it was extremely hard. The situation was about three steps above awkward and she just didn't have a good feeling about it. Cameron had even managed to see Keith, her secret lover, about five times in the last couple of weeks and she loved it. Her reasoning behind her shenanigans was that she wasn't having sex with her fiancé Malcolm yet… so she needed her fix. She thought about how long she and Keith had been*

sneaking around and what caused her to say yes to Malcolm after

only three months of dating. He actually asked after only being

together for only two months but she never would give him an

answer.

She finally agreed to marry Malcolm when Phebe told Keith she was

pregnant with his child. He proposed to her immediately, like the

next day, which crushed Cameron. It didn't matter that Keith had

been begging her for two years to go public with their relationship.

She still felt like he belonged to her, and was highly pissed that he

gave that bitch a ring! The coin flipped when he found out she had

agreed to marry that Malcolm clown, he was even more pissed that

his trophy would soon be passed. They both knew what they were

doing could not last forever but neither one of them wanted to let go.

It just felt so absurdly right.

She snapped out of her thoughts and mumbled, "It's not like I have

much of a choice." Toya, who was standing nearby, heard the

comment and said, "Oh you have a choice! You're a grown woman

who has to live with this decision. YOU HAVE TO LIVE WITH IT

CAMERON, NOT YOUR DAD!" while rolling her eyes. Toya is a

fool but a joy to be around because she will keep you laughing with the foolishness that comes out of her mouth. She stands at five feet six with shoulder length hair, pretty brown eyes, and smooth caramel skin. Cameron and Toya worked part time together a few years back while in high school at a local restaurant. She's that friend with no filter. She means well, but sometimes most people wish she would just shut up because they don't want to hear her honest truth. She gives advice, but her ass is secretive as hell when it comes to her personal business.

"I still can't believe you marrying this nigga without seeing what he working with." That was Shay. Shay was the freak of the group, but you wouldn't know it because she played the innocent role quite well. She had men eating out of the palm of her hands like she was feeding them gold nuggets. They loved her five foot six frame. She was petite with a dark cocoa skin complexion, brown eyes, and her hair was waist length and naturally wavy. She drew men to her effortlessly, but let it be known that she was taken even though she flirted back freely. You would never know who she decided to get a sample from until it was over. That was if she decided to tell at all.

Cameron stood and started pacing the floor. She avoided eye contact with everyone, especially the three girls who knew her darkest secrets. She was still in shock that she was about to get married herself, but she knew she could not disappoint her dad. This reason alone left her no choice. Cameron started screaming, "Not only did my dad plan this wedding, he financed it as well. Oh and I AM getting married in four hours or you hoes will be planning my funeral, so y'all chill out and let's get this shit over with."

It was actually Cameron's dad who had introduced her to Malcolm. One of his coworker/friends knew Malcolm and bragged about how nice of a guy he was. "He's a decent, upstanding, and hardworking young man. I don't want you with any thugs. I think this guy would be perfect for you," her dad told her the day before she finally agreed to meet Malcolm. Daddy dear had begged her about five times before she finally agreed to go on a date. *One date can't really hurt* is what she told herself in order to go through with it. She never wanted to disappoint her parent's, especially her dad, so she agreed to go on the date and one date only.

Cameron knew that each of the girls were all thinking the same thing. They had begged her to rethink this whole marriage ordeal.

They told her to give it more time and get to know Malcolm better. Toya called her a damn fool for marrying someone after only three months of dating. Shay told her she was a got damn fool for not seeing what the nigga was working with. *What if he got a little dick and his sex is wack? What you gonna do then?* She remembered Shay asking her those questions one day at lunch. She looked at each of them and briefly thought of things that they had previously told her, but thoughts of the night before started to consume her mind. The only thing she wanted to do was return to the night before and make a magic wish that it would never end. What was supposed to be a fun filled night with her girls ended up being the complete opposite, but she wouldn't change the events even if she could.

The Night before the Wedding...

Immediately after rehearsal, Cameron walked outside and saw the black car that remains parked at her house through the week. The make and model was a black Dodge Challenger, but it sat there looking as suspicious as a Phantom. You couldn't see through those windows for shit. She bolted to the car and jumped in and it sped off with the quickness. At that moment she wasn't thinking about the rehearsal, the original plans she had with her girls for the night, or her husband to be… Malcolm.

Malcolm was about five feet eight with dark skin and a decent smile. He hit the gym up often and was very muscular though a six pack was nowhere in sight. It was his charm and security that sealed the deal for her. She still couldn't believe she was about to marry him because she was never attracted to dark skin men. This was something totally new to her and she hoped that she could get used to it.

When that text message came through last night that read COME OUTSIDE, the only thing on her mind was the sender…Keith. She couldn't resist his six foot athletic build, smooth caramel skin, and sparkling perfect white teeth. The brother had a smile no woman on earth could ever resist! Let's not forget about his rippled six pack that could compete with any NFL champion. Cameron loved rubbing her hands all over that body of his. She told herself that she would figure out a way to explain everything later, but at that moment she only wanted to be in the arms of her forbidden fruit and nothing or no one could stop her. This would be her last night with him, so she had to make it special. It would definitely be a night to remember.

They shared a relationship off and on, mostly off for about two years. The two of them could never be exclusive because Cameron's dad would not approve of Keith's lifestyle. Her dad remembered Keith because he used to hang out with her older brother Fred before he was forced by their dad to join the army. No one in her family knew about her relationship with Keith. Fred would kill them both if he would've known, and that was a fact. Several text messages suddenly came through all at once:

Sonya: Where are you going Cam?

Toya: Where the hell are you running off to? You really bout to ditch us heifer?

Shay: Really Cam? We done planned this shit for you and you running off?

Toya: If you are with Keith you need to rethink your life…your whole life!!

Toya: You gon give us our money back!!

Shay: Well you better believe we gon still get our money's worth with or without you! These strippers been paid for.

Then a message came through from Malcolm, her fiancé.

Malcolm: Have fun babe! You will never have another bachelorette party.

He has no idea just how much fun I'm about to have, she thought. She knew calls would be coming through next, as well as about a hundred more text messages so she powered her phone completely off. She didn't want or need any distractions for the remainder of the night.

Keith had been driving in complete silence. He finally broke the ice when he said, "You know you don't have to go through with this bullshit. I will go legit and be all that you need. I got you. I don't know how many times I gotta tell you that," he said while staring straight ahead, eyes locked on the road. She could tell he was becoming angry. Cameron could not find the right words to say, so she leaned over and started kissing him as if her life depended on it. First his lips, then she moved down to his ears and neck. He had on gym shorts so it was very easy for her to slip her hands inside his shorts to greet her anxious friend. Keith mumbled in hesitation, but she ignored his pleas and took as much of him as she could into her mouth. He let out a moan and grabbed her hair with one of his hands. She moved her head up and down slowly, enjoying the sounds he was making while trying not to climax and keep the car on the road at the same time. They made it out of town and were coming up on a back road so Cameron told him to pull over and turn off the lights. He did as he was instructed and she immediately pulled up her dress, slid her thong to the side, and climbed on top of him. She began to kiss him passionately as he filled her insides with all nine of his inches. He pulled her dress over her head, ripped her black lace bra off, and began sucking and biting each of her breasts. He gave each one the same amount of pleasure while she continued to move wildly up and down on his thick dick. Cameron was focused on reaching her climax and getting round one out of the way. Her every intention was to totally and completely have her way once they reached his house which was in a remote place out in the country. His fiancé was out of town working, so tonight would be special and stress free for the both of them. *Our last night* rang in Cameron's head which made her sulk in her soul. She immediately shook those thoughts away as his semen filled her and she focused on the matter at hand. Keith. Once they reached his house the first thing Cameron spotted when she walked in was a picture of Keith and his fiancé on an end table. *She was only his fiancé because she faked being pregnant and her dad threatened Keith. I hate that bitch,* Cameron thought. As if reading Cameron's thoughts Keith said, "You could and WOULD be the one I'm marrying if you would just follow your heart and stop worrying about money." Keith walked into the bathroom and Cameron decided to dismiss her thoughts once again as she made her way down the hall. She effortlessly glided to the master bedroom and bathroom, but not before purposely knocking the picture of Keith and Phebe off of the table and shattering the glass frame. Phebe was a five foot five thick girl, but she wasn't fat. She was just thick in all the right places and always rocked a short hair style with various colors. The different hues complemented the hazel contacts she loved which she felt blended so well with her creamy cocoa skin tone. She was the complete opposite of Cameron so Cameron often wondered what it was that Keith liked about her.

Cameron looked into the cabinet and pulled out her favorite bubble bath, some tea light candles, and a lighter to set the atmosphere. Her plan was to take a hot bubble bath, relax her mind and body, and enjoy Keith for one more night. After tonight she had plans on sharing her body only with Malcolm. The thought was painful, but she was going to give her marriage her all. She sank her body deep into the hot bubble bath and relaxed. She thought about calling Keith to join her but decided she would have all night to cater to him…so she enjoyed her bath alone.

Once her bath was complete, Cameron only had one thing on her mind and that was to finish what she started in the car. She dried off and wrapped the towel around her naked body before making her way into the bedroom. For a brief moment she wished she had one of her new lingerie sets from Victoria Secret with her but then decided it wasn't really important. She knew good and well that it would have been off in a matter of seconds if she would have put it on anyway.

Cameron found Keith lying in bed fully naked and aroused waiting for her. He had music playing softly in the background so she knew that he planned on taking the driver's seat for the remainder of the night. One of their favorite CD's was playing. Twelve Play. *You just gotta love that CD* Cameron thought while smiling. Keith motioned for her to join him and instructed her to lie face down. He grabbed the Aromappeal sensuality massage and body oil that she loved so much and began to work his magic. He started at her neck, shoulders, back, legs and caressed down to her feet without missing one inch of her tight body including her ass that he loved so much. He placed sweet kisses on every spot as well. He then flipped her over and gave the front of her body the exact same attention as he gave the back which caused her to moan in pleasure. "Damn bae, that feels so good," Cameron told him.

Keith reached to the nightstand and grabbed a piece of ice from the cup he had placed nearby while she was relaxing in the tub. He used the ice to sensually trace a path down Cameron's body and followed the trail with his tongue. The temperature change heightened the pleasure along with the anticipation of her wondering where he would go next. Keith grabbed another piece of ice and drew circles around her breasts before slowly working his way toward her nipples. When he reached his destination, he sucked them with so much intensity that Cameron was propelled into complete ecstasy. She grabbed his head with one of her hands, letting him know to stay right there for a minute. He inserted two fingers into her pussy while he sucked her breasts. *"Oh my God!"* she cried out.

Keith traveled down further and escalated his ice escapade game. He was enjoying it as much, if not even more than Cameron was. When he reached her pussy, he rotated between sucking her clit with the ice and his mouth and tongue. Back and forth with just the right amount of pressure applied. Cameron immediately climaxed but Keith wasn't done satisfying her yet. After she came again he gave her what she really wanted, and what he knew she was going to miss the most. He fucked her so hard and good that she came three more times just in that round. That was just the beginning of what he had in store. He made sure this would be a night to remember as he entered her raw once again. After declaring that they would always love each other through sweat, tears, and a night full of lovemaking…they both ended the night by climaxing together.

Chapter 2

Three Years Later

If it were not for the three carat diamond ring, wedding photos, and constant stories from Cameron's friends and family, she wouldn't have known a thing about her wedding day. It was all a big blur; there was only a mist where the memories should have been. The ceremony started almost two hours late because Cameron wouldn't emerge from the bridal quarters. She had ice cold feet. It took her dad coming to get her for her to change her mind because wouldn't budge for her mom or her friends. The mentally perplexed beauty imagined the entire ceremony to be just like her life was, routine.

Toya teased her often about not reciting every line in her vows. Cameron literally stared at the pastor on parts she didn't want to repeat like she was in a trance. Toya went in on Cameron about it every chance she got. The entire bridal party was shocked to hear that her husbands' first name wasn't Malcolm, including Cameron. The preacher asked Cameron if she took Keegan to be her lawfully wedded husband and Cameron screamed "WHO?" *That preacher really wasn't supposed to even marry y'all asses. Did y'all attend marriage counseling?* Toya always said.

He despised his first name; therefore he used his middle name, Malcolm. The girls would never let her live that day down. They constantly reminded her that three months wasn't nearly enough time to know enough about a person, let alone marry them. Malcolm vowed not to have sex until marriage so Cameron's father was immediately impressed. He did everything in his power to make it happen, including footing the whole bill. Cameron's mom however was against the entire idea. She never revealed to Cameron that she knew about her secret lover, but she knew everything and she really liked Keith better than Malcolm. She fussed daily saying that Cameron had plenty of time before thinking about tying herself down for the rest of her life because she KNEW her daughter. A bigger wedge was formed between Cameron's parents because of this wedding. She wasn't even twenty-one and here she was about to get married.

Malcolm was so predictable. Cameron knew him like the back of her hand; at least she thought she did. To people on the outside looking in Cameron had it made, but she felt empty on the inside. She only wanted to be truly happy and even at that, more spontaneous. She read so many books with happy endings and envisioned her life to be the same. A bed of roses is what she wanted. Cameron had always fantasized about one of those happily ever after endings and couldn't get them out of her mind. It was her dream.

The newlyweds lived in a 3500 square feet, four bedroom traditional home with three and a half bathrooms. Cameron was able to have some of the amenities she not only needed, but simply desired in her home. She had a spacious walk-in closet, a shoe rack that was to die for, her own vanity, a walk in shower, and a Jacuzzi. She wasn't very hard to please. She liked nice things, but material things were not what she longed for in life. She tried her best to be happy but despite of it all she was miserable. Though she searched her mind and soul, she just couldn't figure out what was missing. She didn't know Malcolm enough to marry him, but she didn't want to admit that to her friends.

Putting all her dreams on hold to cater to a husband and child at such an early age was not what she had dreamt of. Cameron had big dreams of being a famous attorney and getting away from the small town she was raised in. There were no lawyers in her family and she wanted to be the first one. She wanted to move away and make her people proud of her. Everyone was always in anyone's business but their own and never wanted more than complacency in life. One thing Cameron would never forget was where she came from, but she always wanted to do something different. She felt things may have been better if she would've had time to enjoy her marriage for a few years without a child but the cards didn't fall that way. Cameron loved Kingston with all of her heart, but she felt trapped at times. She must have gotten pregnant two days after her wedding. Yes, two days because she did not consummate her marriage on her wedding night.

Sex was nowhere near Cameron's mind the night she got married. A huge argument quickly changed her mind and thoughts. Malcolm made sure to badger her about what went down the night before the wedding, and in her mind she knew he had every right. He had heard rumors about her leaving with some man in a black car and confronted her about them just as a new husband would do. Cameron ignored his rants and to deflect her guilty stance she argued with him about not disclosing his real name. She also brought up the mean stares she received from his family and how ugly the wedding pictures were bound to turn out because of his mom hiring a bootleg photographer. Even though Cameron's dad had paid for everything, Malcolm's mom had taken over with the planning. She changed things as if it were her wedding and attempted to save money that wasn't even hers. She probably pocketed what she saved which Cameron made sure to express to her parents. Cameron slept at her parent's house that night, in her childhood bedroom, and Malcolm slept outside on the porch. He refused to go home without her, and she refused to let him in. Her dad tried to make her go with Malcolm but she continued to refuse, so he finally gave up going back and forth with her about it. She wondered all night if she had made the biggest mistake of her life. Deep down, she knew that she had. Her truth made her cry herself to sleep on what was supposed to be the happiest night of her life.

Malcolm worked as a cross country truck driver and his schedule required him to be gone for two weeks at a time. He would come home for four days, leave right back out and worked overtime when he felt like it. He often complained about being away from Kingston so much, but had yet to put in the effort to find another job. Even though Kingston was the complete opposite of Malcolm from looks to personality, Malcolm loved him with all of his heart. Kingston had a creamy beige skin complexion with curly hair when his mom let it grow out. Malcolm hated for her to let it grow. Everyone loved Kingston so much because he was easy to please and he had a smile that could light up the darkest room.

Cameron was forced to stay at home and raise Kingston until he was school age because Malcolm wouldn't have it any other way. She argued her point constantly but nothing she said mattered to Malcolm. When he told her that he would quit work altogether or find a job at home she finally agreed to stay at home in order to keep him on the road. She was even forced to put school on hold for herself to shut him up. She started to resent him back then because he never compromised.

In the beginning, Malcolm's ways seemed sweet and innocent and Cameron mistook it for true love. Now the word "controlling" pops into her head and assaults her pride when he suggests, or better yet "demands" things. As soon as Kingston became school aged, Cameron found a job as a paralegal. Malcolm wasn't happy about it, but Cameron paid him no attention because she had lived up to her end of the deal. He reminded her about being submissive but she wasn't hearing that shit. In a way, she was on a subliminal strike. To help smooth things over Malcolm had suggested they go to a few different groups at church for newlyweds, oh and he loved to throw things in her face that they heard while they were there. When she threw something in his face he would always make up some bullshit excuse to flip it. Cameron felt like those groups should have been for eighty year old couples, not twenty year olds because the stuff was based from the 1930's. To ease her own mind, or at least mask over her discontent of the whole situation, she decided to focus on her career.

With the schooling and training that Cameron had, as well as a hook up from her friend Toya, she landed the job with ease. She looked at this as an opportunity to be closer to her original dreams. *You gotta crawl before you walk,* she told herself. Cameron absolutely loved her job and it was at work where she was able to relax and be herself.

When Malcolm returned off the road everything was always the same as it has been for the past three years. He would always send a message letting Cameron know how far away he was in the middle of the night. Upon his arrival he walked in the door and went straight to bedroom. After he undressed and showered, he would nudge

Cameron to wake her up. She always pretended to be asleep, but that never stopped him. Before she could even react to him he was in and out of her in the blink of an eye. *If I would've fucked him before I said I do, I never would've married his ass,* Cameron thought. *Damn I should have listened to Shay,* she always thought. No hey baby, no foreplay, no kiss my ass, no nothing. A few pumps and he was always done.

 By the time Cameron finished her shower and got dressed Malcolm was sound asleep, snoring. On that particular morning while Cameron was applying her makeup she heard Malcolm's phone vibrate. That was very out of the ordinary because he never puts his phone on silent. After she finished putting on her favorite lipstick, MAC's Ruby Woo, she walked over and picked up his phone. Even more shocked to find a pass code on the phone, she immediately attempted to bust it. She tried his birthday and BINGO!! *So simple minded,* she thought. Cameron read the newest text message which said, *I enjoyed you, see you soon* with two smiley faces. The number was not saved but it only took a couple of seconds to program it into her mind. Everything else had been deleted except messages between Cameron and Malcolm, plus a couple from his mom and sister begging for money. He was still snoring when Cameron placed his phone back down with her mind was racing a mile per minute. She had never gone through his phone before and began to feel like it was a mistake to do so at that time. *I would rather not even know,* Cameron thought. *Who is this woman that enjoyed my husband so much that she just had to text? How long has she been texting? Time will surely tell,* she thought as several thoughts began to take over her mind. She started to wake Malcolm up but decided against it when she glanced at the clock. She still needed to cook breakfast before she left for work. She always left food for him to prove that she could work while maintaining her household duties. It didn't stop him from making smart remarks, but she did her part which put her mind at ease.

Chapter 3

As Cameron drove to work after dropping Kingston off at preschool, she tuned into the Rickey Smiley Morning Show as they were doing a segment called Love and War and a thought entered her mind. Malcolm is cheap and would fall for anything free so he could easily be persuaded, but Cameron wouldn't allow herself to be embarrassed in such a manner. She continued listening in as the woman talked about how she suspected her husband was cheating and why she felt that way. She had them to call his cell phone and offer him a free trip, making everything sound legit. Once he agreed to take them up on their offer they asked him to provide a name of who would be accompanying him. The husband asked a few questions and then told them that he would be taking a woman by the name of Monica or something. They beeped out the last name. Go figure, the woman whom he had named was not his wife but a coworker as he revealed. His wife couldn't hold her composure even though she had previously been asked to do so she made it known that she was on the phone. All hell broke loose. She cussed him out from A to Z and pig Latin back and forth! The husband began to stutter and try to convince her that he was just playing along with the people on the phone but the wife wasn't hearing it. He even tried to say that he knew she couldn't get off work and just wanted to show his new coworker a good time. She told him that he better go to the Monica bitch house after work because he sure as hell would not be able to come the place he used to call home.

Just as quickly as the thought entered her mind, she dismissed it. Cameron began thinking, *No way in hell would I embarrass myself like that. Maybe I'm over thinking this. Surely it's nothing. I've been faithful, loving, caring, understanding, and totally committed to him since the day I said I do. I'm sure he's satisfied. The only time we argue is about me working. He still wants me to sit at home but that is not up for debate. What man doesn't want a woman who is bringing something to the table in this economy? Sure he makes good money, but I don't want him holding it over my head like he has before. If I want to buy myself something nice I don't feel like I should have to jump through hoops to explain myself. He pays bills for his mom and sister every month without even consulting with me so I will continue working to bring something to the table and of course stashing some away in my rainy day fund. Every woman better keep a stash just in case because you never know when a nigga is going to trip. Oh and we argue about the fact that he wants to have more kids right now but I feel like we are content. I told him if it happens it happens, but he'll never know my birth control pills are the reason it hasn't happened yet. I've never complained to him about not being satisfied sexually so that can't be it. Shay put me on to something that helps me to get the edge off and it has helped me to remain faithful.* The only time she could enjoy sex with Malcolm was when she thought about Keith. She knew how wrong that was but it was only for a few minutes anyway which made it at least tolerable to do.

Cameron made it to work, her place of peace, and logged into her computer before starting a fresh pot of coffee. She bumped into her girl Sonya, who was a junior partner at the firm and smiled while saying good morning. Sonya complimented Cameron on her red and white Versace blouse then immediately began to bash her about not meeting up with the girls for drinks on Saturday night. Cameron didn't even have the chance to tell her how nice she looked in her orange Donna Karan dress that complimented her skin so well because Sonya was going in on her. Cameron had met Sonya through Shay and they were all mutual friends of Toya's. Toya and Shay both worked as occupational therapists across town.

Malcolm hated for Cameron to go out with anyone so she always made excuses not to go with the girls unless they could all take their lunch breaks at the same time or meet up immediately after work. Sonya gave her usual speech about how Cameron needs to enjoy life because we only get one, and silently she agreed. *Don't let life pass you by and honey live yo life,* were phrases she would say often. Sonya is married with a little boy and she still finds time to have a social life which is why she's always preaching her point. She was pregnant with a little girl but lost the baby at five months, so she took that as a sign not to have anymore. Even though her parents and in-laws loved kids and wanted her to try again, she didn't want to put herself through the agony of possibly losing another child. In her eyes no one understood the pain that she felt. She never really expressed herself much but she made it clear that she was content with her son. Cameron always took Sonya's words to heart because deep down she knew she was right and was genuinely trying to help. Sonya was a few years older than Cameron so she felt like Sonya was someone she could look up to. Cameron genuinely liked her and was glad they crossed each other's paths in life. Cameron agreed not to miss the next outing because if her feelings were accurate about what happened with the phone from this morning, she would definitely need a drink or three and some girl talk. Probably even some shots.

Cameron started thinking back to how Malcolm use to run her bath water, rub her feet, give her massages, buy spontaneous gifts, and take her out. She thought back to their very first date and how sweet Malcolm was. She didn't want to go out with him in the beginning and she felt guilty for her thoughts after seeing how sweet he was. He was a true gentleman. He pulled out her chair, ordered for her, and was very attentive which was something she had never experienced before. Cameron was impressed but she still couldn't help but to think about Keith, the one love that she no longer mentioned. She hadn't realized it until now, but all of that had stopped some time ago. She had been able to remain true to her word that the last time would truly be the LAST time. It had been almost a year actually. *How could I not notice that? I guess going through the motions does that to a person,* Cameron thought.

SHIT, Cameron swore mentally. She had been daydreaming and not paying attention so the coffee had run over and spilled onto her hand, blouse, and thigh. She didn't even notice that she had started crying. Sonya walked back by and was ready to continue with her bashing until she saw the tears and disturbing look on Cameron's face all the while noticing her coffee stained blouse as well. "Cam what's wrong?" Sonya asked sincerely. Cameron began to cry harder feeling like she was losing her mind with her many thoughts. It seemed as if an ocean was enclosing itself around her mind. Sonya grabbed some Kleenex and paper towels and passed them to her. Cameron thanked her and tried her best to assure her that she would be fine. She explained that she really had a weird morning and she honestly didn't know how to express it at the moment. She honestly didn't know what to think so she figured it was best to keep quiet instead of jumping to conclusions. She took a few deep breaths and promised not to miss the next outing with the girls so that she could relieve some of her rising stress. Sonya gave her a gentle hug and told her that she would see to it that she kept her word before rushing off to a meeting that she had scheduled. Cameron was thankful she kept a change of clothes in her car most of the time, because now she didn't have to leave work and go buy anything.

Cameron turned on her radio at her desk and was able to make it through the day without any further incidents. Listening to music was always relaxing to her and she loved all types. It was just her thing. When I'm not Gon Cry by Mary J, Blige came on, she sang her little heart out on the verge of tears but some kinda way she held it together. The very next song was Get Low by Lil Jon and The East Side Boys which changed her mood instantly out of the funk she had been in. She filed all the documents that had been handed down to her, sorted through cases, and conducted research for the current cases she had been assigned at a robotic speed. She was beyond busy and loved the distraction and satisfaction that it brought to her. Malcolm would never understand how much she loved her job or the reasoning behind her dedication to it. On the flip side, he never tried to understand either.

As the day came to an end, Cameron grabbed her things and said her goodbyes to everyone. She decided to order take out from Malcolm's favorite restaurant because she wasn't up for cooking today, so she called in an order right before she left the office. She ordered them both eight ounce rib eye steaks, baked potatoes, and house salads from Harvey's. Kingston would enjoy his favorite, a burger and some fries. She could have easily grabbed that from McDonald's but she only wanted to make one stop. As Cameron drove to pick up the food she sent Malcolm a text to let him know her plans because he would have a million questions if she was late, especially on a day he picked Kingston up.

As soon as she sent the text and put her phone down it vibrated. She picked it up expecting a reply from Malcolm, but instead she read a text from an unknown number that said, YOUR TIME IS ALMOST UP!!! "What the fuck?" Cameron said out loud. She decided to call the number instead of texting back but got no answer. She called five times but no one ever picked up the phone. She sent a couple of text messages since no one answered and waited for a reply. Nothing came. Cameron was ready to fuck someone up and she knew she needed to start with Malcolm, but she wanted to get whoever had been texting him first because she was pretty sure it was the same person who had just texted her.

Chapter 4

Two Months Later

Things had most definitely taken a huge turn in Cameron's life, and not for the better. She began to catch Malcolm in more and more lies. He even started coming home from work without texting her, but she knew which day he was coming because she kept up with his schedule herself. She didn't have anything to hide so it didn't matter to her one way or the other about him not texting. Whatever he thought she was doing was just all in his crazy ass head. He always accused her of cheating, it had become a weekly debate and she was tired of it. He didn't know how close she was at times but she had been true to her vows so far.

When she confronted him last month about the text messages she saw on his phone and even the one she had received a couple of months ago he acted like it was nothing. She even saw more messages but remained quiet in order to build her case. He told her that if the number wasn't saved in his phone then someone must have texted the wrong number. He even tried to flip the message she received on her by saying someone must have been after her for something she had done! He once again accused her of fucking around. She told him he must have been the one cheating since he was always accusing her. She almost told him if it wasn't for the bullet she had, she probably would have been cheating but she bit her tongue.

In the midst of their arguing Cameron's phone rang and she immediately recognized it to be the number that had been calling and texting Malcolm. She silently wished she was wrong but her gut was telling her that all hell was about to break loose. The very first message that started all of her problems, *I enjoyed you see you* soon, with those two got damn smiley faces was one she couldn't forget even if she tried. She was already pissed the fuck off so she answered the phone with an attitude by screaming "WHO THE FUCK IS THIS?" The female on the other end of the phone said, "Malcolm and I are in love and he's leaving you to be with me!! I'm tired of us having to hide and you don't love and appreciate him the way he deserves. He made a mistake marrying you, it should have been me. I even love King"…that was all the caller could get out before Cameron snapped. "LISTEN YOU BITCH DON'T YOU DARE LET MY SON'S NAME COME OUT OF YOUR MOUTH!! WHO THE FUCK ARE YOU!! WHERE THE FUCK ARE YOU

BECAUSE AFTER I FUCK MALCOLM UP PLEASE BELIEVE I WILL BE FUCKING YOU UP AS WELL!!" The female revealed her name to be Nikki and was trying to apologize for things unfolding the way they did but was cut off again by Cameron. "Nikki Johnson from around the corner?" Cameron began to feel weak. *There is no way in hell this motherfucker went and fucked this trailer park trash right in the same town,* Cameron thought. She wasn't able to say anything else because Malcolm ran up and grabbed the phone from her before throwing it against the wall shattering it to pieces. "YOU LOW DOWN STUPID ASS DUMB ASS BLACK MOTHERFUCKER! YOU FUCKING THAT TRASH ASS BITCH THAT LIVES IN THE TRAILER PARK?" Cameron screamed. "How could you do this to me?" Tears streamed down her face and she felt her anger level rising higher. She didn't want to cry, especially in front of him, but she couldn't stop the tears no matter how hard she tried. She screamed and cried, then scream some more. Cameron called him every name that she could think of plus a few she even made up. "You got your bitch threatening me and then you got the nerve to try to blame me? You must be out of your rabbit ass mind you low down dirty son of a bitch!" She totally forgot that Kingston was there watching and listening to every word but she couldn't control her anger.

The argument was so intense that night that it turned physical. Cameron broke pictures, even wedding pictures. She broke a TV, shattered an end table, threw several random objects and attempted to burn some of Malcolm's clothing. She wasn't successful with burning anything because he restrained her at that point and she was overpowered. Not giving up her rage, she scratched his face and drew blood so he began choking her. He had both of his hands wrapped around her throat and was squeezing with all of his strength. Cameron felt her world fading away and was fighting to stay conscious. He was choking her just that hard! She had her nails as deep into his skin as she could get them because at this point she was fighting for her life. He was telling her to let go but she wouldn't. She knew at that point he had lost his everlasting mind because HE was the one choking HER! The house phone began to ring but they both ignored it. Kingston was crying and screaming at them to stop but they both ignored him as well. They were still literally at each other's neck. Cameron was finally able to gather some strength after Malcolm made a move when the phone rang again so she brought her leg back as far as she could kneed kicked him in the nuts. He screamed and immediately released the grip he had on her neck to grab his balls. She started coughing uncontrollably but was finally able to get up from of the floor.

A few minutes later, there was a knock at the door. It was two of the neighbors, nosey ass neighbors at that. After she completely broke away from Malcolm he headed towards the front door limping. She seized the opportunity and grabbed her car keys before heading towards the back door. She heard Kingston crying for her but she was unable to physically or emotionally comfort him at the moment. She needed to get away from the chaos before someone died in front of her son. She didn't want him to witness a murder and be scarred for life. Malcolm turned around to see that she was trying to escape and rushed in her direction with fury in his eyes but she picked up a lamp off the other end table and threw it directly at his head before he could reach her. This made him stagger and she noticed a knot immediately begin to form. She saw blood so she used this opportunity to continue making a run for her car. "AS SOON AS MY BROTHER COMES HOME HE'S GONNA FUCK YOU UP

YOU BLACK MOTHERFUCKER!" she yelled and slammed the door.

Cameron only had one location on her mind and that was to get to Nikki Johnson's house. She didn't consider Nikki to be a friend or anything but they always spoke to each other in passing. Nikki always prolonged the conversations they shared which she always thought was odd, but nonetheless thought she was cool since she wanted to talk. She had figured that the woman just probably didn't have any friends to talk to. *I can't believe this motherfucker,* she thought to herself. Cameron was seeing red and she couldn't think straight for shit. While she was driving she drifted back to a time in her life that she wanted to forget. *Anger that Cameron thought she had buried years ago was beginning to rear its ugly head. She started thinking back to the many people who had wronged her and the different acts of revenge she used. She would be in jail if anyone would've known the exact details. Many speculated, but no one could prove anything. Cameron drifted back to her sophomore year in high school. Throughout all of her years in school up until the last two she was the dark skin, skinny, pimple faced, unattractive (in her eyes) girl who wore glasses. She never had a boy so much as to even look at her. There was one boy that she secretly liked but he hung out with one of the guys that always picked on her so she never even entertained the idea of approaching him. She received ridicule from boys and girls constantly and she never even bothered a soul. Cameron was on the basketball team, and it was in the locker room where the prank started that pushed her over the edge. Despite being a loner, Cameron was a decent basketball player and her coach even encouraged her to run track. He told her it would help to keep her in shape year round along with other things so she agreed. Her dad loved that she participated in sports; he never missed a game and recorded just about everything she participated in. He was her number one fan.*

After practice one day, Cameron was the last person to walk in the dressing room. She didn't have curves like the other girls so she purposely stayed behind to shower last. Some days she waited until she got home to shower, but on this particular day she was very sweaty and needed to stop by the store before going home. She couldn't skip taking a shower that day. She was tired of being picked on so she waited later and later each day trying her best to avoid the girls.

When she thought the coast was clear, she hurried out of her clothes
and made her way to the shower. Upon reaching the shower floor
Cameron slipped and before she realized what had happened, she
saw cameras flashing everywhere. One girl even had a bottle of baby
oil in one hand and her phone in the other snapping pictures. Her
name was Brittany. She tried several times to get up to no avail so
she finally just sat there looking and feeling humiliated. She refused
to shed another tear in front of these stupid ass girls. They had
followed Brittany's lead and played tricks on her before but never to
this extent. That humiliation lasted for about fifteen minutes but it
seemed like an eternity.

She went home that night and cried herself to sleep without telling
her mom or dad what had happened. They never understood where
she was coming from when it came to matters like these. Her dad
assumed everyone loved her, and her mom was simply always busy.
She tried talking to Charlotte, her sister, but she said that she
probably was just the victim of a senior prank and shrugged her off.
Charlotte never even stopped to say those few words; she just spoke
her peace and kept walking without missing a step. Cameron felt like
her sister didn't like her so she didn't confide in her much anyways

and this was the perfect example of why. She was always stuck up under her man of the month's ass so she rarely had time for anything else. Cameron suspected that Charlotte didn't like her because she was used to being the baby, but their parents treated them all the same so she never understood the cold shoulder her sister always gave her. Charlotte even let two girls jump on Cameron while she was in junior high but luckily Cameron held her own and kicked their asses. Charlotte gave her the excuse that she knew she could handle them but Cameron wasn't buying it. If two girls would have jumped on her sister, she wouldn't have thought twice about jumping in to help her. They were like night and day and Cameron was slowly trying to accept the fact that her sister hated her. Her parents would always say Charlotte didn't hate her and make excuses for her but Cameron was tired of the lies so she started facing reality.

If only her brother Fred was at home. He was a hot head for sure but he was also the one person who always had her back no matter what. Fred graduated two years prior and because of his constant mishaps with the law their dad made him enlist in the army. He consistently hung with the wrong crowd and trouble seemed to always find with him ease. At first he was upset about being forced to join the military, but he eventually grew to love it. She missed her brother so much, this day proved why she kept things to herself. She cried herself to sleep that night and tried to fake a sickness the next morning, but her mom was not buying it. She made her get dressed for school and told her she didn't want to hear anymore fuss about it. When Cameron made it to school she noticed the weird looks and laughs that she started receiving from everyone. She wanted to turn around and run away from school, but she continued to drag one foot in front of the other. When she made it to the hall near the cafeteria, she saw pictures hanging on the walls and doors. The closer she walked the clearer they became. They were pictures of her lying naked on the floor in several different positions. The pictures from yesterday had become her worst nightmare come true today. The most shocking picture of them all was the picture with Arnold, the school nerd, lying naked with her. Cameron couldn't understand how or why anyone could or even want to do this to her. She had never been around Arnold naked. She started fuming on the inside as people continued laughing and pointing their fingers at her.

At this point, she could only turn around and run. She ran straight to the gym where no one would be at this early in the morning. It was right then and there that she decided she would stand up for herself and take matters into her own hands. She began to mentally put her plans together. Cameron got up after about two hours and headed out the door. She didn't care about the absentee mark that she would get for the day. She would come up with something to tell her parents whenever they brought it up. She had shed enough tears and her tears were getting her absolutely nowhere. She wasted no time putting her plans into action. Her parents would be gone to work by now and she would have easy access to her dads shed. All she needed were a few tools from the shed, and a trip to the store to gather other necessary supplies. Her grandmother worked in the cafeteria so she knew just what to do in order to complete phase two of her plan. Phase one would require more manual labor, but she was willing to put in work that night. She had watched her dad change enough flats and work on enough cars in her spare time to be able to do what she had in mind.

Cameron thought back to how the "accidents" played out, leaving Brittany dead from a car accident, two of her friends in critical condition, and pretty much the entire school with either diarrhea or vomiting...some both. Detectives said that something went wrong with Tiffany's tires and that it was just an unfortunate accident. No foul play was ever suspected, by the authorities anyway.

Cameron took pride in her revenge and it was even sweeter that no one could prove what she done. It was scary that it was so easy to implement what she had visualized, but she had no remorse. Not one ounce. Things turned around quickly for her after that. People began befriending her and it gave her a sense of confidence. Brittany's friends later came and apologized to Cameron for following Brittany's lead and putting her through so much hell. They told her that they didn't realize what they were doing at the time and if they could take it back they would. She talked her mom into letting her get contacts and also made an appointment to a dermatologist who corrected her skin problems. Cameron became more active in social activities, and even worked out and lifted weights outside of her mandatory sports regimen. She even started dating. She didn't like to think about her boyfriend much because it made her cry. He was killed in a car accident about a year after they started going out. The two had become the school's favorite couple and his accident almost shut Cameron completely down. She would forever cherish the memories she shared with him. Keith came into the picture later but she never considered him to be her boyfriend.

Being told that time heals all things; she began pulling herself together after the loss of her boyfriend. Along with the help of counselors and friends, she was able to heal up pretty nicely and even gained more confidence. She felt like she was the shit again within a couple of months after the accident and took a turn for the better in her eyes. One thing she had vowed to do was leave her anger tucked deeply away forever. Who would've known her husband would be the one to cause those old feelings to resurface.

It only took Cameron about ten minutes to reach her destination. On the short drive over all she saw was red while reflecting on the past and present. She could not think of one reason why would Malcolm mess with someone in the same town they lived in. And then he picked a hood rat with four kids already and rumor had it that she was pregnant again. She shook her head and tried to calm herself down but it was pointless. She just couldn't understand his logic. She had given Malcolm a chance when everyone else only used him. He shared with her about his past relationships and she felt bad that he had gone through those trifling women. Everyone he dealt with in the past only used him for his money. She never asked him for anything and he found that to be strange which made him shower her with gifts often. She was so hurt and confused about everything that was going on it almost made her sick.

Cameron clearly wasn't thinking logically at all because when she turned into the driveway, instead of slowing down she pressed the accelerator down to the floor and ran straight into the house. Her airbag popped out and her windshield glass shattered. She sat there stunned not really realizing what she had actually done because she was clearly an emotional wreck. She never noticed the cuts that were bleeding on her face and arms. She sat there frozen until she heard kids crying and screaming. She started to feel a little bad for them but not for that bitch Nikki. It registered what she had just done and she had hoped that she would have run over Nikki with the impact. Her attempt was unsuccessful which worked out in her favor in the end. Nikki quickly gathered her kids and ran out of the house yelling and screaming. She had no idea what had just happened but as soon as she noticed Cameron she started cursing her out. A few of her neighbors had walked outside and started looking to see how the scene would play out. Some had their phones out recording because they KNEW it was about to go down. Nikki charged toward Cameron but when she saw Cameron rushing toward her with fire in her eyes, she started running the other way. Cameron caught up to her and just as she grabbed her by the hair and yanked her someone grabbed her arm. "LET ME GO, LET ME GO!!" Cameron screamed. They picked her up and told her to calm down. Cameron tried to break loose from the man but she couldn't. All she wanted to do was beat the fuck out of Nikki.

The next week Cameron was sitting at a table with her girls filling them in on the story. She was on her third amaretto sour and felt like she needed more than that to help numb the pain so she ordered a shot of Patron. She rubbed her neck at that very moment reminiscing on Malcolm choking her. "That black motherfucker really choked me," she said under her breath. She still couldn't believe that things had escalated so quickly. He really put his hands on her when he was the one who was in the wrong and had gotten caught. He had called his mom and her parents after Nikki had called him to tell what Cameron had done. Nikki also called the police. Cameron told them about the argument she had with Bertha, Malcolm's mom. She refused to call her mother in law after she got called so many bitches by that woman on that night. While Cameron was in the police car she heard Bertha say, "That baby don't look like my son anyway. I been telling Malcolm to get a blood test because I know you're an undercover hoe who is only using him for his money." Licks would have been passed and probably so much more if it had not been for the police already being there. Cameron yelled at her calling her an ugly old bitch that needed to find a man of her own. The verbal altercation between the families was just as bad as all of the other events from that night. She told them how she had no regrets even as she was taken to jail in the back of the police car. She was thankful that her mom had taken Kingston to her house before she was handcuffed and put in the car. Her heart would have broken more if he had witnessed that. Her son he had seen more than enough between her and Malcolm on that night and the past months as well. "I went into the cell but only stayed an hour or so because Malcolm paid for all of the charges upfront. He also paid to fix that bitch house, the temporary living arrangements while the house was under construction, he paid her to drop the charges, and bought me a new car," Cameron said. Sonya, Toya, and Shay were all sitting there listening to her while visualizing a lifetime movie. "So you married this nigga after only knowing him for three months, a female called you and said that your husband is leaving you to be with her, he attacks you, y'all fight, you run your car through this girls house which could've caused you more bodily harm as well, his mom cusses you out, tells you that she doesn't believe her son is Kingston's father, and you go to jail. Does that sum everything up?" Toya asked. "Oh and I know I've asked this before, but is Kingston REALLY Malcolm's son?" Toya asked with side eyes. "Yes he is," Cameron answered for the hundredth time. Sonya couldn't quite find the right words to say at the moment so she remained quiet. "And the sex is wack," Shay said while shaking her head. She continued by saying, "I can't believe you've been married for three years without cheating and your husband can't make you bust a nut. I know you're glad I took your ass to Fantasy Land and hooked you up with those toys or your ass would be crazier." The look on her face was a look of pure disgust and pity. "Are you sure you haven't dipped back to Keith because there is some reason Malcolm is acting an ass," Shay continued.

"NO I HAVE NOT," Cameron answered while looking aggravated.

"Honey, what is it that you want? Living in dysfunction is not normal," Sonya said finally finding her voice. She continued by telling her that she shouldn't subject Kingston to all of this. He is young but children pick up on things very quickly these days. The girls were all asking questions but noticed that they were overwhelming Cameron so they all backed off. Shay changed the subject by mentioning an upcoming concert and asked if everyone was interested in going. Everyone showed interest so Shay said she would look up the ticket information.

"I wish I would've married Keith," Cameron said immediately changing the subject back to where they attempted to escape. "I know he really loves me because he hasn't even married Phebe yet." All of the girls shared the same thoughts but remained quiet so that they wouldn't make her feel any worse than she probably already did. She continued, "I cut him completely off for this bullshit. The next time he reaches out to me, I'm not going to ignore him like I normally do. This is some bullshit I'm dealing with and I know that he can and will help me."

Toya spoke up by saying; "Don't make the situation worse by starting something new before ending what you have." Cameron didn't pay her any mind. She was use to the lectures given by her friend but at the present moment she was fed up and ready to get even. *Whatever happens just happens* is what Cameron thought to herself. She sped their gathering along, said her goodbyes, and left with her mind on sweet revenge.

Chapter 5

One Month Later

Cameron sat in marriage counseling twiddling her thumbs. She was

letting everything go in one ear and out the other. It was not only

because she didn't want her marriage to work; it was because

Malcolm was just putting on a big front for the pastor with his lies

and crocodile tears. She wanted to slap his black ass.

 She was also unmoved because the same pastor conducting their

counseling session had tried to hit on her and many other women she

knew of several times before. He tried to get her number in slick

ways at church, and when he was unsuccessful with his attempts he

sent Facebook messages to her. He even had a baby by one of the

members of the church! Despite the fact of his infidelity, his wife

still showed up with him every Sunday on his arm like everything

was peaches and cream in her Easter looking suits and Sunday hats.

That's not even half of it. He was having an affair with one woman

who was engaged but ended the affair about two months before her

wedding day. He officiated the wedding, and resumed the affair two

months after she had been married. *I guess two months is his grace*

period, she thought while shaking her head. He was most definitely a do as I say and not as I do type of pastor and Cameron had no more respect for him. She didn't even come to his church anymore unless Malcolm begged her, but it wasn't often that she gave in. She just couldn't stomach that man much. She wanted to slap his ass too and kick him in the balls. *Sure he is only human, but instead of making excuses, he should own up to his mistakes and stop putting everyone else down,* Cameron thought. Because of this, she chose to go to her family's church no matter how boring the services were because the people were genuine.

She told Malcolm about what he had done and how uncomfortable she felt being in his presence but he brushed her off and insisted on using his pastor and not talking to a complete stranger. "A complete stranger won't be biased," she had argued with him but it was pointless. His mind was made up. That was another slap in the face to Cameron and she was starting to resent Malcolm even more than she wanted to admit. She also felt like he was the one with a problem so she shouldn't even be going. He could sit in counseling and cry and lie without her as far as she was concerned.

During the session her phone was vibrating like crazy in her purse and Malcolm asked who kept calling her. "It's probably just Toya," she lied, although she wanted to cuss him out for even having the audacity to ask. She knew exactly who it was. She had told him where she was going and he wasn't too happy about it. He didn't hide his anger about it either. "You need to go on and leave this clown ass nigga," he had told her. He just didn't understand that it wasn't that simple. She would make it up to him later, she thought while smiling devilishly.

She focused back in on Malcolm telling the pastor that he did not cheat; he was just talking to the girl. He said that he would never cheat on his wife because he loved her. He was saying how badly he wanted to make his marriage work and how he knew Cameron was the woman for him from the first time he laid eyes on her.

Cameron interrupted by saying; "So you really expect for me to believe that this bitch called to tell me that you are leaving me to be with her off of your words alone? You telling a damn lie. You done fucked her and you know it. Your conversation ain't that good. Save that bullshit!"

The pastor carefully interrupted her and asked, "Will you watch your language please Sister Cameron?" She shot him a look, and if they could kill he would be headed to meet his maker at that very moment. He straightened his tie, cleared his throat, and shifted uncomfortably in his chair but continued speaking by asking Malcolm what led him to communicate with another woman? "I... I... I don't know," Malcolm stuttered and began to cry even more. "It just happened, but I didn't sleep with her," he continued. Cameron was completely turned off by his tears and fakeness. *I married a fucking clown. He's so weak and pathetic,* she thought. Cameron was quiet throughout the remainder of the session. Even when she was asked a question she remained quiet because she knew that nothing nice would come out of her mouth. "Do you love your husband? Do you want your marriage to work? Are you willing to forgive him and ask for forgiveness for things that you have done?" The pastor asked several more questions but Cameron remained quiet. She was over this session way before it started. She eventually wrote them a note saying those exact words so that they both would stop asking her stupid questions and expecting her to respond. It didn't work. They continued trying to include her but she cussed them both out and they finally got the hint. Hell, she even fought the urge to take her phone out during the session while they continued to talk about nothing.

The pastor finally ended the session and then asked them to join hands for prayer. Cameron reluctantly obliged after being asked three or four times. The only thing she heard was Amen. After the pastor closed out, he told them that he would like to meet with them again in a week for another session. The following week he wanted to start meeting with them separately to try and get to the root of things. Malcolm hurriedly agreed but Cameron immediately declined. She made it known that she would not be seeing him again but he and Malcolm could feel free to conduct their sessions without her. Malcolm announced that he was willing to drive back home from work for the session, but she remained unbothered. Her decision was final, she was not changing her mind and she wanted to kick her own ass for agreeing to come in the first place. She wanted to curse them out again but instead just simply said "Good day devils," and walked out while waving her hand like she was Miss America.

Malcolm made it to the car about fifteen minutes after her so she had time to respond to her text messages and make a phone call while she waited. He asked her if she wanted to pick Kingston up from her parents and go out to dinner. She wanted to say hell no and request to go straight home, but she thought about him only having two days left at home and decided to play nice to keep the peace. *The quicker these two days pass by the quicker I'll be free,* she thought. "That sounds fine," she finally replied. There were times in the past when she just wanted to spend time alone with Malcolm, but he acted as if he was married to Kingston at times. His actions eventually wore her out, so now she didn't care one way or the other in that area.

After they picked Kingston up they headed out to dinner without exchanging words with one another. The atmosphere was so solemn that Cameron fell asleep on the way; when she woke up they were at Kentucky Fried Chicken. Cameron was thankful when Kingston told his daddy he wanted pizza because she did not want anything from KFC. They ended up at Pizza Hut a few minutes later. Cameron let Malcolm place the order because she knew he was going to make a fuss about the ticket either way it went. Sure enough he did. He knew good and damn well what all he ordered but it never failed. Cameron shook her head in reflection about Malcolm not being the man she first met, the man who use to shower her with gifts. She even had to leave a tip because he got up without leaving one. She shook her head quickly in complete disgust. Cameron let Kingston do all of the talking for the night. She was just ready for Malcolm to hit the road and head back to work.

As soon as Malcolm left going back to work two days later, Cameron was headed to Keith's house, wasting no time dropping Kingston off with her mom beforehand. Though her mom had been questioning her whereabouts lately, she hardly ever refused to watch Kingston because she loved her grandbaby with all of her heart. He was her only grandchild and he looked like her twin with a light skin tone and curly hair. The only time she didn't keep him was when she was already out during the times Cameron would call or stop by. She pretty much knew what her daughter was up to without her telling her.

For the past two months she had been seeing Keith as often as she could. It was kinda awkward to reach out to him after ignoring him for so long, but she finally found the nerve to make the phone call. She was a nervous wreck wondering how he would respond, and had waited a whole month before actually dialing his number after she had made up her mind to do so. It seems that everything was meant to be because when she called Keith, he and Phebe had just had a big argument that led her to stay at her parent's house for a few days.

Cameron smiled at her luck as she listened to him vent about their problems in a bout of frustration.

Keith told her how much he loved and missed her and she began to pour her heart out about what she had been through. She told him that she made the biggest mistake of her life by marrying Malcolm. She said that she did love him, but she wasn't in love with him. "This is all my dad's fault. I should have listened to my mom. I never fully trusted Malcolm. There was always something in his eyes but I ignored it," she continued. Keith told her that he had been hearing about some of the things that she had been dealing with. "Who told you?" She asked.

"The streets always talk, and no matter the location I stay in the know. I'm gonna always protect you no matter what bae," he said. "I'm sure my brother keeps you in the know since y'all hang around in the same circles. When is the last time you talked to him anyway?" she asked.

"It's been a minute… but yo, check this out, I need you to go out of town with me next weekend," he said. "I need to make a run," he continued.

"Where she gonna be at?" Cameron asked while slightly rolling her eyes.

"I don't know and it don't even matter," he replied while kissing her. He ignored her slight attitude because he had been missing her like crazy. Cameron agreed while thinking all she had to do was tell Malcolm she was going out of town with Toya. She had used Toya as an excuse so much lately that she decided she better start telling her just in case Malcolm decided to call her. She didn't care about Malcolm's feelings but she knew she had to be smart.

After they finalized their plans for the next weekend they continued to express just how much they had missed each other's touch over the last three years. Cameron apologized for ignoring him all those times he had reached out. She let him know that she was really trying to do right and she didn't want any drama, or to lead him on for that matter. He told her he understood and returned to kissing her. They devoured each other while trying their best to make up for lost time. Words couldn't explain how much they had missed each other. He pinned her hands above her head with one hand, and with his other hand he brought her face to his and stroked her tongue erotically with his. She felt his erection growing by the second and she was already soaking wet. He pulled at her black lace panties while she lifted her hips to give him better access to pull them off. He yanked them off and threw them on the floor in one swift motion. He then pulled his blue polo boxers off and his dick sprang free. A smile spread across her face and her pussy pulsated even more. She closed her eyes and gasped as he entered her slowly, inch by inch until he filled her insides. He started stroking at a slow pace and then developed a smooth rhythm as she met him thrust for thrust. She pulled him closer to her and wrapped both of her legs around him and cried out in pleasure. He grabbed her left leg and put it over his shoulder and stroked her deeper. After about ten minutes they both climaxed together and lay in each other's arms happy and satisfied. That was only the beginning of making up for lost time.

Chapter 6

Two Weeks Later

Malcolm had begun to fuss more and more about his job though he loved what he did and made more than enough money to support his family financially; but he felt like he needed to be at home with his family. He had a pretty hefty savings as well and felt like he could quit and still be OK. The only thing on his mind was wanting to be a family again so he constantly apologized to Cameron for the Nikki incident. She said she had forgiven him but they both knew that was a lie because it was clear in her actions.

When he came home she purposely put Kingston in the bed with them to keep from having sex with him. As a cover up, she lied saying that Kingston had been having nightmares. Kingston played right along with her enjoying his moments of not having to sleep alone. He had even slept in the bed with his mom and Keith last weekend and was getting back use to not sleeping alone.

On last week, Cameron had allowed Keith to come over for dinner and Kingston took to him instantly. They even played games and watched TV together. Cameron noticed how extremely happy Keith was with Kingston but she also noticed the sadness that was deep within his eyes. Keith had shared with her that he had taken care of a child for two years only to find out that the child wasn't his. The day he found out about his alleged seed, he was there to visit and to drop off shoes, clothes, and toys without hesitation. He had spent the whole day with the child only to bump into his real father on his way out the door. There was no denying the resemblance but he had to ask the question anyway. He stared the dude up and down and the room went cold. The mother of the child stood there frozen in one spot until the real father spoke up. She knew the kind of men that they both were so she finally snapped out of her trance and stood between the two of them. Keith knew that his gun was in the car and he saw the guy put his hand on his hip so he knew what time it was. He was no punk by a long shot but he wasn't stupid either. He just went ahead and left.

 It turned out that the mother of his supposed to be child had been playing both men. Keith's mom insisted that he get a DNA test so that he would never have to wonder what if. He took her advice and his thoughts were confirmed. He was crushed. He had fallen in love with the little boy and wanted to remain in his life but couldn't deal with the constant drama that it would bring about. He also didn't want to confuse the child so he removed himself from the situation completely. It hurt him deeply.

His current girlfriend or "fiancé" had told him that she was pregnant; he was ecstatic but it was short lived because it turned out to be a false alarm. Cameron believed that she had been lying the whole time but there was no way she could prove it. Keith didn't want to believe that Phebe would lie to him about something like that. Cameron stopped bringing it up because she was tired of him defending the bitch. With all of his pent up emotions now on his sleeve, Keith started treating Kingston like he was his biological son. Neither of them realized what they were really doing.

Later that night Keith said, "The connection I feel with Kingston is so strong. I've never asked you this before, but is Kingston my son?" Cameron had never entertained that idea at all and Malcolm's mom was the only person who ever questioned the paternity. "No, I wish he was yours bae, but I'm pretty sure he's Malcolm's," she said. They both dropped the subject but silently shared their own thoughts. She knew she had been with him the night before she got married but figured she didn't get pregnant then.

Cameron was brought back to the present when she heard Kingston asking her about "Unk"? She had told him that Keith was his uncle but never thought he would ask for him, especially in front of Malcolm. "He's probably at home baby," she said and quickly asked him if he wanted some candy attempting to change the subject. "Who is Unk?" Malcolm asked. Cameron tried to ignore him but he asked again so she hurriedly said "He's just talking about my cousin, he told Kingston to call him Unk," before Kingston could say anything else. Kingston was looking confused and looked like he was about to say something else so Cameron scooped him up and went into the kitchen to avoid Malcolm's glare. She knew that she was wrong, but in her eyes he started it so she felt like *oh well, it is what it is*.

After dinner, she gave Kingston a bath and put him to bed. After he was sound asleep she went and cleaned the kitchen then prepared herself to hop in the shower. "I hope you don't have a headache tonight because I'll be waiting up for you," Malcolm said as he winked. She turned her back to him and rolled her eyes. Before she stepped into the steamy shower she opened the medicine cabinet and grabbed a couple of Tylenol PM's. She threw them down her throat and washed them down with a little water from the sink. *Maybe I can sleep through his few minutes again,* she thought.

It was becoming normal for her to pop pills for any and everything. She had mentioned taking pills to Toya who told her to be careful with taking over the counter medications so frequently. Toya's concern made Cameron limit telling her much about it. Cameron stepped into the shower and the hot water felt so good to her skin. She immediately began to reminisce back to last weekend's trip with Keith. Malcolm had blown up her phone nonstop but she didn't allow him to spoil her mood. She acted like her and Toya were just shopping and visiting her cousin, trying to downplay her excitement when she really was having the time of her life. He made it known that he wasn't pleased about her trip, but she told him that she didn't want Toya to make the trip to Atlanta by herself. Keith had bought her more shoes, clothes, and a new Gucci bag on top of it all. She had taken a shower with him the morning before they returned home, so she decided to think about that so that she could bust a nut before leaving the steamy oasis because she knew it wouldn't happen until she saw Keith again.

When she finished her shower she dried off, wrapped up in a towel, and said a silent prayer that Malcolm had drifted off to sleep. She had purposely stayed in the shower until the water turned cold in hopes that he would grow tired of waiting and just take his ass on to sleep. She slowly opened the door and sighed when she saw him wide awake naked in bed waiting for her. "So much for that prayer," she mumbled to herself.

As she walked towards the bed she decided that she would try a different approach. She slowed her pace and did a catwalk to the bed. She couldn't remember the last time she kissed him so her plan was to at least try to enjoy this and make it last. She thought about the time she tried to go down on him before and how he had acted a complete fool. *Surely he's grown up by now,* she thought. She let her towel drop to the floor to expose her tight body and perky B-cup breasts just before she made it to the bed. She bent down and started kissing him. "Let's make this a night to remember bae," Cameron said. He tried to say something but she put her finger to his lips to silence him and continued with her foreplay. She planted more soft kisses on his lips, ears, and then moved down to his torso. His body tensed up and she told him to relax. As her kisses moved further down and she grabbed his dick, he hopped up and screamed "WHAT ARE YOU DOING?" She was immediately agitated and said I was trying to spice up our sex life. "What grown man doesn't want head, especially from his wife?" She asked.

"Decent and respectable women don't do those things. Only drunks, sluts, and whores do that and you better not be either one," he replied. She just stood there frustrated. She was so turned off by him and his actions and was fighting very hard to keep her mouth closed. She knew that once she started talking she would really hurt his feelings, and no matter how it looked she really tried not to do that. Trying to understand him was not working, and to be honest she was really tired of trying. She decided that the best thing to do at that moment was to lay down, let him get his few pumps in, and turn over and go to sleep. She had already gotten hers in the shower so it really didn't matter anyway.

Chapter 7

Cameron didn't know it was even possible, but she had fallen deeper in love with Keith. She was in that head over heels, wanting to cook and clean, have his baby and all that kinda shit type love. She was doing things with him that she had only read about in books and dreamed of. When they were able to sneak away, they dined at some of the finest restaurants and he always bought her things as well as broke her off with cash. She stashed most of the money because he was gonna always buy her something anyway. She truly wished that they could be with each other explicitly but couldn't figure out a way to make it work. With both of their significant others working out of town it was easy for them to practically live together, and that is exactly what they were doing. It was working out so well that they never thought about the consequences their actions might cause. They were just living life carefree.

One evening, they were lying on the couch watching TV when out the blue Kingston asked, "Do I have two daddies?" Cameron and Keith both stared at each other in shock, neither of them knowing how to respond to him. You could hear a pin drop it was just that quiet. Cameron finally found her voice and said, "Why would you ask that baby?" Kingston explained that one of his friends lived in two houses like they were doing and said he has two daddies, so he assumed he must have two daddies too. "This is Unk and Malcolm is your daddy. You only have one daddy ok?" Kingston seemed pleased with the answer and went back to watching TV and playing with his toys. Cameron made a sigh of relief and lay back on Keith's chest.

He was silent but he still wondered if there was a chance that Kingston might be his son. Cameron's cell phone started ringing. She was pretty sure it was Malcolm. Every time she left home now she would forward calls from the home phone to her cell because calling the house phone was his slick way of checking to see if she was at home. Before she answered she whispered to Kingston, "We are at home watching TV," because she knew Malcolm was going to ask him. She picked up the phone and Malcolm started talking about how tired he was being out on the road and away from home. Cameron sighed because she knew where this conversation was going but she didn't want to give him a reason to come home so she held her composure. Malcolm knew that Kingston was about to start playing tee ball which made him want to be at home. Cameron put on her good wife act and told him that she knew it had to be hard on him but he couldn't just up and quit without having another job. She really didn't think they would make it together if he was home every day. She told him that he wasn't missing much and she would start recording more things for him. She down played everything he said in attempt to make him feel better about missing things.

He asked her to pass the phone to Kingston. "Hi daddy," he said. Malcolm asked him what he was doing. "Mama said we are at home watching TV," Kingston answered. Cameron's eyes got big as saucers and her mouth flew wide open. Her heart dropped to the floor when Keith's phone rang loudly in the background because she was positive Malcolm heard it. Keith jumped up to answer it to keep it from ringing more. Cameron tried to think fast on how she was going to get out of this. Kingston got up and walked towards her with the phone stretched out. "Yes bae," she said.

"Don't yes bae me. Why did Kingston make it sound like you said to tell me y'all are at home watching TV and who's phone is ringing in the background? It sounds like a house phone but I called our house phone. What's going on? Where y'all at?"

When he finally stopped talking, she said, "When the phone started ringing I said daddy always calls when we are at home watching TV so Kingston was just repeating what I said. Oh and that's Toya's phone you heard in the background. She stopped by to bring me something. Cell phones have all kinds of ringtones you know," she added. It sounded like his phone beeped so he said he would call her back. She didn't realize she was holding her breath until she hung the phone up. She briefly wondered who was calling that made him drop that argument so quick. Keith walked back in with a worried look on his face. "My mom said that Phebe just left her house so let's go to your house," he said. His mom knew what was going on and did any and everything she could do to protect her son. Cameron knew deep down his mother didn't care for her, or the situation they were in but she always looked out for her dear son. *Thank God she stepped in today because I'm not trying to get caught up in this house, especially with my son,* Cameron thought while gathering her and Kingston's things. She looked in the kitchen and saw all of the dirty dishes in the sink that they used to eat spaghetti and garlic bread with and thought about going to wash them real quick but changed her mind. *She can wash our dishes for us,* Cameron thought to herself with a smirk.

The next day at work Cameron was smiling from ear to ear. She had received two dozen roses with a card that read, *May these roses brighten your day just as thoughts of you always brighten mine. Love always, bae!!* Cameron was ecstatic. Keith was definitely her bae and she knew she was his too. Malcolm had never sent roses to her job. He never sent anything period. He didn't even want her to work so it wasn't a big surprise that he never did. These were sent just because, and that made them that much more special. Keith had cooked breakfast for her and Kingston that morning and had left her with some outstanding good morning sex. The sex was way better than the French toast and eggs in her eyes. She could have Keith for breakfast, lunch, and dinner without getting tired of him. The roses topped off her morning. He was meeting them at the park later that evening for Kingston's first tee ball game. Cameron knew that they were both in way too deep but how could she stop it? It felt so good. She loved every minute of it.

Around 9:30 she received a group message about meeting up for lunch at The Grill around 11:45. She confirmed then set her reminder for 11:30 and got busy with her case. She was currently working on a personal injury case and was having a hard time obtaining full medical records from the hospital. Normally when this happens someone is trying to hide something so she knew she would have to make a trip to the medical records office at the hospital next week. She would do all that she could but knew it was highly unlikely to get the information she needed for it to be a Friday, so she added a note on her to do list for Monday morning. She was thankful for the connections she had made while on the job, because of those connections she knew things would always flow smoothly when she needed certain documents or anything.

While Cameron was still hard at work her phone started beeping with her lunch reminder. *That was the quickest two hours ever,* she thought to herself. Sonya was walking towards the front in her fierce navy blue skirt suit and Jimmy Choo shoes to match. Once she got near Cameron's desk, Cameron asked if she wanted to ride with her.

"Suurree I'd love to ride in the new Camaro," she replied.

"I'll trade you my car for your wardrobe. You look great," Cameron said to Sonya.

"You look great too girl, but when you wanna make the deal?" Sonya said laughing before hopping in the passenger seat. Malcolm called while they were headed to the restaurant. Cameron didn't want to answer his call but she knew he would only keep calling until she answered so she decided to go ahead and get it out of the way. Sonya noticed how dry Cameron was with her responses but decided to check her Facebook and Instagram. She kept her thoughts to herself for the time being. When Cameron got off the phone Sonya finally let out the laugh she was holding in from the some of the Instagram posts she was looking at. After a few more minutes they pulled up to the restaurant at the same time Toya and Shay pulled up. "Wooo don't y'all look great today. Y'all tryna catch new men at work?" Shay said to Cameron and Sonya. They laughed thanked her before heading inside.

Once they were all seated, Toya and Sonya ordered waters while Cameron and Shay ordered Dr. Peppers. "I love your Vince Camuto bag Toya. That yellow is beautiful," Sonya said.

"Thanks boo," Toya told her and sat back in her chair. "Malcolm texted me and asked did we enjoy ourselves in Atlanta," Toya said smartly while cutting her eyes at Cameron. "You know it would be wise of you to inform me when we're doing things that I know nothing about in advance, don't you think?" She continued.

"I meant to text you but I got caught up and forgot, my bad," Cameron replied.

"Mmm mm you must have been out of town with Keith again. That boy got your mind gone," Shay said.

"Someone by the name of bae sent her to work with the biggest smile ever and she also received two dozen roses," Sonya added.

Cameron filled them in on everything that had been going on. She saved the part about them practically living together and Kingston calling Keith Unk as well as his plans to come to Kingston's game for last. They all stared at her in amazement with their mouths opened when she finished. Of course Toya was the first to reply.

"Have you lost you damn mind girl? OMG!! You can't be serious Cam!! You are playing with fire honey!! You know that husband of your ain't playing with a full deck"

"That must be some great sex. I just said that boy got your mind gone but I see he got every damn thang gone. Goodness," Shay said.

"You can't expect for a child to know when and when not to talk. I can't judge because no one is perfect but you gotta keep the baby outta this,' Sonya said while sipping her water with lemon. Cameron was hearing them but she wasn't listening. "I'm not judging you either, but can you use a little more discretion? I heard you ate lunch with Keith at Pap's Place," Toya said.

"Isn't that place downtown, in your hometown?" Sonya asked.

"Yeah," Cameron shrugged. "People don't really be paying attention though," she added. 'Girl, people are ALWAYS paying attention," Shay said.

"Well he started this. If his bitch would've never called my phone I would've never started back seeing Keith. Y'all just don't know how it feels for somebody to lie to you and have you looking stupid," Cameron vented.

"Yes we do," they all said in unison.

"Well Cam, I know you don't always like to hear my mouth, but when anybody comes to me with a problem I give my honest opinion. I might as well not say anything if I'm not gonna keep it one hundred. I've known you long enough to know that you're gonna do what you wanna do anyway so I'm not even gonna lecture you today, but I think I can speak for everyone when I say just be careful. You really are playing with fire, and if you continue someone will eventually get burned," Toya said.

"Yeah, because you doing some killing type shit. People snap out when they find out this kinda shit," Sonya added. Cameron listened and was glad she left out the part about giving Keith a key to her house. She could hear Toya's mouth in her head right now just thinking about it.

Chapter 8

Malcolm had been holding the phone listening to fussing and begging for the last ten minutes. This current phone call was the complete opposite of his last one. This one turned the big smile he had after listening to that sexy voice from the last call into a big ass frown. He hung up the phone with his mom tired and frustrated. "I can't ever give her enough money," he said to himself. He loved his mother dearly and she had protected him in so many ways that he felt like he had to do everything she asked, but he was getting tired. He had also grown tired of his mom saying that Kingston wasn't his child so he was trying to decide how he could go about getting a DNA test. He didn't want to drag her down to the clinic or anything so he was trying to come up with a plan. He knew that Cameron was going to flip out on him because she had asked him if he wanted a blood test when Kingston was born. By her getting pregnant so soon, to the world it seemed like she was already pregnant before they got married. She pretty much insisted that he get a DNA test so that there wouldn't be any problems in the future. She had noticed the stares from his mom when Kingston was born, and she even heard a couple remarks because he was light skinned with curly hair. *Baby we don't need no kinda test, I know that's my son. Forget about what everyone else says or thinks. It's all about us,* he had assured her. After that discussion, they both agreed to never bring it up again and they held to it. They pushed it out of their minds. Now here he was about to cause all hell to break loose. "This is going to make her go crazy but I'm tired of hearing my mom's mouth," Malcolm said to himself.

He had just took an exit and stopped at a rest stop so he decided to get out of his truck to stretch, use the bathroom, and go grab a snack and a drink. He walked up to a complete stranger at the vending machine and started venting about his dilemma. The stranger was taken aback by his straight forwardness but listened in closely. Malcolm even said Cameron and Kingston's names a couple of times. The stranger suggested that Malcolm go ahead and get the DNA test if it was what he needed to do to ease his mind.

"Do it for you, not your mom the stranger," said before walking off. Malcolm felt better after confiding in someone who didn't know anything about him or his family personally; or so he thought. Malcolm decided he would look up the information and get this taken care of immediately. *Better late than never,* he said to himself.

Chapter 9

Cameron danced around in her room while getting ready for the R. Kelly concert that she was going to later with her girls. Shay had mentioned the concert a while ago and they all agreed to go enjoy themselves. It would be a great distraction from her drama filled life is what Cameron had told herself. Malcolm would be home later that night and he was supposed to pick Kingston up from her parent's house. He made a smart remark about her going but didn't put up a big fuss like he normally would have. Cameron wondered what that was about but decided not to even entertain it. She was just ready to enjoy herself.

Keith even had something smart to say about her going out, but he was going somewhere with Phebe so Cameron told him he better chill out. She didn't bother to tell him where she was going once she found out he was taking Phebe somewhere, and neither did he which was fine by her. Keith was starting to show more and more of the signs that Cameron saw in Malcolm and hated. She saw the signs but ignored them.

She had taken Kingston to McDonald's to play in the balls earlier then dropped him off with her parents. She was looking forward to this night out. She tried on a couple of outfits then called Toya and asked her what she was wearing. Toya told her she had decided on a black jumpsuit with a red blazer and red Jessica Simpson heels. "I'm still undecided and you know I can't wear heels," Cameron whined. "Umm, if you can balance two men I know damn well you can balance some heels," Toya laughed and said. They chatted for a few more minutes then hung up so they could both get ready. Cameron decided on a black leather skirt and a cute purple and gold crop top she had picked up from BeBe on one of her trips with Keith. Wedges would have to do because she wasn't wearing any heels and they were even pushing it. She figured she would be cute and comfy. After she finished getting dressed she fixed her hair and applied her make up. She noticed that her favorite lipstick, Ruby Woo was running low so she decided to use a color that the lady at the Mac counter recommended called Heroin. It was a light purple shade and actually blended well with her top. Cameron admired herself in the mirror and was assured that she was cute. She grabbed her MK clutch, cell phone, car keys, checked herself in the mirror one more time, and headed for the door. She came right back to her full length mirror and snapped a couple of pictures to post on Instagram then left.

The girls decided to leave in time so they would be able stop and eat first. They met up in Louisville at Toya's aunt's house and parked their cars. Shay was rocking a blue jumpsuit with some nude Jessica Simpson heels, and Sonya was killing it with her all black dress that showed off her curves. She was rocking some bad black and gold Giuseppe Zanotti heels. Each of the girls were looking hot and was sure to turn plenty of heads. Shay called a stranger over to take a group picture of them, then she took about two hundred selfies.

Cameron drove to Jackson from Louisville. Malcolm called Cameron saying that he would not be able to make it home until tomorrow night. Cameron wondered why and wanted to ask, but she didn't want to argue with him so she just said OK and called her mom to let her know not to wait up for Malcolm. She didn't mind keeping Kingston overnight anyway. The hour and a half ride was smooth and laid back with old school jams blasting and them talking shit to each other. Cameron's wedding seemed to always be the topic they got the best jokes from. She was use to the jokes by now and laughed right along with them while adding her own to the story.

Once they made it to Jackson all of the restaurants were packed so they decided on the least crowded one which was Red Lobster. It wasn't too far from the coliseum so it turned out to be the perfect spot. They had their endless shrimp special going on so Toya was very pleased with the restaurant choice. They were seated in a booth, looking over the menus when the waiter came to take their drink orders. Everyone ordered a soda, even Toya and Sonya since it was the weekend. "Toya who are you texting while you cheesing from ear to ear?" Sonya asked.

"Honey her secretive ass ain't gon tell you shit," Shay said.

"Will y'all hoes shut up and mind ya business," Toya said while finally putting her phone down. Cameron read a text message then immediately started looking around. "Shit," she said. "What is it?" Shay asked.

"Keith is somewhere in here with his bitch. He just texted me," Cameron said.

"Oh lord," Toya and Sonya said together.

"This is supposed to be a drama free night," Toya continued.

"I didn't know they were gonna be in Jackson this weekend. I didn't even tell him where I was going after he told me they were going out," Cameron said.

"Does Phebe know what you look like?" Shay asked. Cameron dropped her head and told them that she thought Phebe found a picture of her in Keith's phone. "I got a couple of phone calls from an unknown number after he told me about it but I never answered. That's been a few weeks now." Cameron continued.

"The nigga keeps pictures of you in his phone? Wow!" Toya said more than asked in amazement.

"Where are they? I wanna get a good look at this man that got you so sprung," Shay said.

"I hope they're not going to the concert too," Cameron said. Toya looked at her like she was crazy and said, "Why else do you think they would be in Jackson?" Cameron rolled her eyes at Toya and said, "Shit, I was planning on having a good time tonight."

"Shiiddd we still gonna have a good time. Fuck all that," Shay said.

"She's staring at you so she knows who you are," Sonya said.

"She's picking up her phone so if yours rings don't answer it Cam. Just act unbothered," Toya said. "We don't need tonight to be the night that she puts everything together." A few moments later Cameron's phone started ringing and she fought hard to keep her composure. "Keith over there looking more nervous than a hooker standing in front of a prophet at altar call," Toya said and laughed. Since Toya and Sonya had the best view of Keith and Phebe, they told the other girls their every move and made mention when they noticed them leaving. Phebe looked pissed the fuck off. The rest of their time at the restaurant was filled with more questions and comments from the girls which Cameron ignored. She was sitting there not knowing how to shake her jealousy. She could hear Toya's voice in her head *saying how you mad and you got a whole damn husband of your own?*

They made it to the concert about thirty minutes before it was scheduled to start and found their floor seats. Shay had found them great seats at a great price. They were turning heads left and right as they walked through heading to the front. A DJ was playing music as everyone continued to make their way to their seats. It felt like a big party so they all relaxed and started having a good time.

A comedian opened up the show with a thirty minute set that had everyone in the building laughing their asses off. "Most comedians that do a set before a concert starts are wack but he was pretty good." Shay said. She saved his name in her phone so she could look him up later. After he finished up, the lights went off and everyone got quiet. A spot light appeared from the back of the room and R. Kelly appeared in the middle and made his way down the center aisle and up on the stage. Every woman was screaming at the top of their lungs because he opened up the show with one of his classics, Bump and Grind. Ladies on the outside row were able to touch him when he walked by. Next he sang Seems like You're Ready, Sex Me, and then Your Body's Calling.

Everyone was having a great time. When R. Kelly sang a song about taking selfies and let women come to the stage, Shay broke her neck and made it up there. She discreetly pushed about three women out of the way and made it on stage and got her selfie with the one and only Kellz. She was so damn happy. When he went into Feeling On Yo Booty, Toya noticed Cameron staring up into the balcony. She followed her eyes and spotted just who she thought she would see, Keith and Phebe. "Forget about him and have a good time tonight," Toya leaned over and whispered to her. Cameron smiled and said you're right. She shook her mood instantly and waved her hands in the air and got back into the music. Cameron then spotted a guy sitting by himself close by and made her way down the row to dance with him. She whispered in his ear and started grinding on him like he was her man. Toya noticed Keith mean mugging Cameron, and apparently Phebe did too because she pushed Keith so hard he fell back into his seat. Cameron started having the time of her life while putting on her show. She knew exactly what to do to make Keith jealous. Mission accomplished.

Chapter 10

The next morning Cameron woke up with a banging headache. She had taken making Keith jealous to the extreme. She ordered more than a few drinks and made the best of her night. She even took a few shots. Toya ended up having to drive home because Cameron was just that damn drunk. Shay was drunk too and Sonya would be sleep before they made it out of the parking lot so Toya got them all home safely. The poor guy Cameron was using to make Keith jealous really thought he stood a chance. He had followed them all the way to the car and Toya had to get ugly with him before he would go on about his business. He didn't leave without calling Cameron a few bitches, but she was in such a good mood and drunk that she paid him no attention.

 Cameron drug herself out of bed the next morning and went into the kitchen to find some Tylenol. She popped three and downed them with some orange juice because she really hated water. As soon as she laid back down the doorbell rang. "Who could this be?" She said. She went and looked out the window and saw a white van with the acronyms DDC (DNA Diagnostics Center) written on it in black and red.

When she opened the door and a white man stood there with the same acronyms that were on the van on his white shirt with a red and black logo. Cameron looked at him confused and asked, "Who are you and what are you doing here?" Before he could answer her mom was pulling into the driveway with Kingston. Cameron glanced at the clock on the wall and noticed it was a little after eleven o'clock. "Damn I was supposed to get him by nine o'clock," Cameron said to herself. The man fumbled with a clipboard and then finally found his voice and said, "A DNA test was ordered by a Mr. Malc"....he couldn't finish the words before Cameron exploded. "WHAT THE FUCK DID YOU JUST SAY??"

"Ma'am, I apologize but I'm just doing my job. I have no control over this. I'm here to perform a DNA test on a Kingston Price," the man said.

Cameron's mom had walked up without Cameron noticing and was standing there listening in awe. She was fuming on the inside because she really didn't care for Malcolm, but she knew she had to keep a level head because she knew how irate her daughter could be. One of them had to be civilized. Cameron stormed into the back to get the phone and called Malcolm about five times in a row but he never answered. She decided to leave a voice message on her next try. "YOU COWARD ASS PUSSY ASS MOTHERFUCKER!! HOW DARE YOU PULL SOME BULLSHIT LIKE THIS!! I HATE YOU! SINCE THIS MAN HAS DRIVEN ALL THE WAY HERE I'M GONNA GIVE YOU THIS GOT DAMN TEST BUT DON'T YOU DARE BRING YOUR BLACK ASS TO THIS HOUSE!! YOUR SHIT WILL BE AT YOUR BITCH ASS MAMA'S HOUSE BECAUSE I KNOW SHE'S IN ON THIS SHIT!!"

Cameron was fuming and shaking uncontrollably. A big crowd had formed in the neighbor's yards and she just wanted to crawl up under a rock and die. "Those nosey bastards have probably already informed the whole county about what's going on," she said. Tears would not stop falling from her eyes so her mom hugged her to try her best to comfort her. "I'm about to call your dad honey," her mom said. "NO, he's the reason I married this fool. I don't want to see him right now," Cameron said.

The man read off all kind of disclosure and privacy rights information that Cameron paid no attention to. Her mom was the one asking all of the questions. The man only answered her mom when

Cameron shook her head that it was OK to respond but she still wasn't really paying attention. Kingston didn't really understand what was going on but he hated to see his mom so upset so he was crying too. Cameron had to sign some paperwork before the test could be administered and managed to scribble her signature. The man performed the test on both of them and gave Cameron a card. He told her that the results would be sent through the mail or whatever method was requested within seven to ten days. Cameron was numb but she took the card and made a mental note to tuck it away safely.

Cameron was emotionally spent after the morning she had. Her mom packed Kingston a bag and took him back with her without Cameron even asking. Cameron hugged and kissed them both and told her mom thank you. "Don't do anything that's going to land you in jail," her mom said before she left. She knew her daughter very well and knew that she was more like her than she cared to admit. Her mom briefly started thinking about some of the things she had done back in the day, in the name of love. Cameron just half smiled then closed and locked the front door.

The first thing she did was call a lock smith. A man showed up within thirty minutes, he was charging double since it was the weekend. Locksmiths show up quick when double pay is on the line. Malcolm still hadn't returned any of her calls and she had no plans on calling him anymore. She wanted to make a pile and burn all of his clothes in the yard, but she didn't want to cause another scene. Her house had been the center of attention enough for that day already.

Cameron went into the kitchen and poured herself a glass of wine, then grabbed the box of trash bags and headed back to the master bedroom. She began pulling all of Malcolm's clothes out of the closet and filling the bags up. She grabbed her cell phone, called Toya, and asked her to come over and help her with something. By the time Toya made it, about twenty minutes later, Malcolm's side of the closet was empty. Toya stood there in shock, not even wanting to ask what was going on. Cameron didn't give her time to ask, she just ran down the morning's events as she drank her third glass of wine. "Is it safe for me to be here?" Toya asked while stepping back and looking down the hall.

"I've changed the locks and I doubt his bitch ass shows up anytime soon. He won't even pick up the phone," Cameron replied. "I'm about to take all of his shit and throw it in his mama's yard," Cameron continued.

"And you want ME to help you? You tryna get me killed too huh? You know Malcolm ass is Looney as hell," Toya said.

"I only want you to drive because I'm about to finish off this other bottle of wine. I can't believe this motherfucker would really do some shit like this. I asked that bastard if he wanted a blood test right after Kingston was born and he said no. I hate him. He pulls this bullshit one week before my birthday at that. He was taking off next week and we had plans to go up to the mountains. He can forget about that shit. I'll get that money back and spend it on myself," Cameron vented.

"Have you heard from Keith today?" Toya asked.

"Nope and I really haven't had time to think about him today," Cameron replied.

"Well, let's find something to do for your birthday next weekend, and since we're talking about birthdays, I'm having my dinner in Columbus at Rueben's this year. Go on and put it on your calendar.

You know I expect you to be there," Toya said. Cameron finished throwing everything in the bag, and asked Toya to help her put everything in the truck. "I thought the only thing I had to do was drive," Toya rolled her eyes and said while picking up a bag. When night fell Cameron was ready to execute her plan. Toya drove the fifteen minutes it took to get to Malcolm's moms house. During the entire ride she tried to talk Cameron out of throwing Malcolm's clothes outside but Cameron wasn't paying her any mind because she was texting Keith. She had told him a portion of what happened and asked him to come and spend the night with her. He told her that he would be there later but he didn't think it would be wise to park his car at her house tonight. Cameron looked up from her phone and told Toya that Keith was going park his car at her house later and she would pick him up. Toya mean mugged Cameron while silently cursing her out and thinking how she has really lost her mind. When they turned the corner and saw Bertha's house in view Toya turned the headlights off. She drove slowly like they were about to perform a drive by or something; it was only a drop off but Toya was nervous. When they got directly in front of the house Cameron hopped out and started grabbing bags and throwing them in the yard.

Cameron reached into the truck and grabbed a lighter and piece of paper and set a few of the bags on fire. She knew it was meant to be when she spotted some lighter fluid in the back of the truck. She poured some on the fire and the flames ignited higher. "What the hell are you doing? You didn't say anything about burning shit girl," Toya said. Toya really had no plans to help her, but she put the truck in park and got out and helped her anyway thinking the quicker they threw the bags the quicker they could leave. She didn't want to get caught there, especially since Cameron started a fire. Toya wanted to cuss Cameron out but wanted to leave expeditiously so she bit her tongue.

 They almost made it without being noticed, but they heard Bertha's mouth before they even saw her. "Oh shit," Toya said, while silently praying Cameron wouldn't react to this woman. No such luck. Bertha called Cameron a gold digging whore, a trifling bitch, and so many other names that had Toya standing there frozen with her mouth wide open. Cameron ran towards Bertha but Toya snapped out of her frozen state just in time to grab her before she got close enough to put her hands on the old woman. Toya begged her not to do anything stupid. Cameron told Bertha that she can have her bitch made son because she didn't want him. She even told her she could have his wack ass dick because she was acting like he was her man instead of her son anyway. Toya shook her head and pulled Cameron to the truck. They heard Bertha screaming something about leave her son's truck there, but Toya sped off and left her screaming to the air. It started raining before they made it to the corner. "I hope all of his shit gets soaked," Cameron said.

"You mean the shit that didn't burn," Toya said as she continued to drive away from that nightmare.

Chapter 11

Malcolm had been calling and texting Cameron for three days straight and she ignored him for every single last one of them. The night after she threw his shit in his mother's yard, after he embarrassed her by bringing a damn DNA truck on wheels to her front door, he came home crying, begging, and pleading but she wouldn't let him in. She told him to go to hell and leave her the fuck alone.

Even if Keith wouldn't have been lying in her bed she wouldn't have let him in. Keith was laying there like he owned the place. He did break Cameron off with stacks at a time so he felt like he was paying bills there too. After two hours of Malcolm being outside, Cameron thought he was finally leaving when she heard a car. Shortly after she heard a car there was a knock on the front door followed by the words POLICE, PLEASE OPEN THE DOOR MRS. PRICE. "Oh my God, what else is gonna happen today?" Cameron screamed. She got up, put on her robe and headed to the front. Keith was right behind her but she told him it would probably be best if he stayed in the back just in case Malcolm tried to force his way in the house. He didn't argue with her, but he didn't really agree with her either. He felt like she had been dealing with enough bullshit and he wanted to be close to her to protect her just in case anything else jumped off, but he stayed in the back like she suggested. He had even let the stunt she pulled at the concert slide, for now at least.

Cameron opened the door and stepped outside to talk to them. Malcolm was a few feet away talking to another officer. She was disgusted by just the sight of him. The officer who had knocked on the door explained to Cameron that since it was both of their house and they were married, she couldn't keep him from coming home. "Sir, with all due respect, I'm letting you know in advance if you all allow him to come back here tonight one of us will be in a body bag by morning and I don't plan on it being me. He just needs to give me some time." Cameron said to the officer.

 "Let me see if I can talk him into giving you some space for a little while, but he's pretty adamant about coming home," the officer told her and walked off. The officers switched positions and the one who had been talking to Malcolm came over and stood by Cameron. It was clear that he understood her position, but didn't want his personal feelings to interfere with his job. "Ma'am, we are going to do everything we can to get him to give you some time to cool off.

You can't legally put him out and eventually you're going to have to face him, but I understand your frustration. A few of your neighbors called in and gave us insight on what has been going on," the second officer said.

"Thank you," Cameron said.

"And just to give you a heads up, you might want to get him some help, he's said some very off the wall things," the officer continued. Cameron just looked at him dumbfounded, not knowing what to say. The first officer walked back over and told her that Malcolm agreed to give her a couple of days to cool off but sent his apologies through the officer and said he was not going to live without her. Cameron thanked the officers, said her goodbyes, and walked back in the house closing and locking the door behind her. She looked out the window and watched as they all left before heading to the back where Keith was waiting.

Cameron was at work filing some papers happy that it was Wednesday and the work week was halfway over. She was sad that she had two days of work left and had no idea how she was going to get away with Keith to celebrate her birthday with Malcolm off work and harassing her constantly. She had put in to be off but she decided to go ahead and work since her plans were ruined. Work had always been her place of peace, but with everything she had going on in her life she couldn't even enjoy her job like she used to.

It was hard for her to sleep and she was having constant headaches so she had gone to the doctor on her lunch break Monday and was prescribed some pain pills as well as something to relax her and help her sleep. She still felt sluggish which was why she was ready to go home. It was almost time for lunch when her cell phone rang and an unidentified number popped on the screen. Cameron didn't answer the first call, but when it rang again, she decided to answer. "Hello," she said.

"We are trying to get in contact with Mrs. Cameron Price," the caller said.

"This is she," Cameron said.

"Ma'am, there's been an accident involving your husband, Mr. Malcolm Price, and we need you to come to Baptist Memorial Hospital," the unidentified caller said.

"What happened? Is he OK?" Cameron asked.

"We think he's going to be fine, but we have some concerns and need you to come down right away," the caller said. Cameron told the caller OK but she was confused and trying to figure out what the hell was going on. She wondered what the hell Malcolm had done now. She gathered herself and went to tell Sonya what was going on and informed her boss about her family emergency before leaving. Sonya offered to drive her. Cameron didn't want to inconvenience her, but Sonya had her purse and car keys out before she could decline. Sonya sent a group text to Toya and Shay letting them know what was going on. They texted her back and said they would meet them there as soon as they finished up with clients.

As Sonya was driving to the hospital, Cameron sat in the passenger seat and was able to check her text and voice messages. She had about fifteen voicemails that she was sure were all from Malcolm. Sure enough she was right. She deleted most of them right after he said a few words not caring to listen to his whining, begging, and complaining. When she got to the last and most recent one she didn't delete it and she screamed "OH MY GOD," when she heard it and scared the shit out of Sonya.

"What the hell is wrong with you?" Sonya asked. Cameron didn't even reply, she just put the phone on speaker and replayed the message. *I miss you and if I can't come back home; I have no reason to live. I love you…* that was Malcolm's voice followed by a loud crash. Sonya now looked as disturbed as Cameron. "Did this nigga try to kill his self?" Cameron asked. Sonya wouldn't dare voice her opinions at that exact moment. She couldn't wait to get to Shay and Toya.

When they made it to the hospital and got inside, Cameron spotted Bertha at the information desk. She silently cursed but decided that she would try her best not to make a scene in the hospital. She was sick of Bertha and wanted to kick her ass but knew it would be best to act as civilized as possible. Unfortunately, Bertha had other plans because as soon as she spotted Cameron she rushed towards her screaming and accusing her of hurting her son. "I haven't seen your crazy ass son," Cameron said before she even realized it. "God is gonna get you. You low down conniving bitch," Bertha said to Cameron. Malcolm's sister did the best she could to try to get her mom to be quiet but security appeared before she was successful. Sonya pulled Cameron in the direction of the information desk to find out what was going on and see where they could find Malcolm. The receptionist slowly tapped on the keyboard and then picked up the phone and made a call. Cameron wanted to snap on her for the funky attitude she was displaying but remained quiet. Within a few minutes, a doctor and a nurse appeared into the double doors and called for the Price family. Sonya had initially decided that she would stay in the lobby until she noticed Malcolm's mom making her way towards where Cameron was headed with the staff. *Cameron is gonna need someone back there with her so I better go,* Sonya thought to herself. They made their way to the back and gathered in a meeting room. Two uniformed officers were sitting in the room and when they all walked in they stood and introduced themselves. Cameron and Sonya both glanced at each other. The doctor was the first one to speak up once everyone but Cameron was seated. She was too nervous to sit down. "Mrs. Price, your husband was involved in an accident that could have taken his life, but since there were witnesses present they were able to call 911 and get him to the hospital expeditiously. It was touch and go for a moment, but he's stable and doing quite well. He has a concussion and a few cracked ribs, but he should heal fine," the doctor said.

"WHAT HAPPENED?" Bertha screamed. One of the officers spoke up and explained that it appeared that Mr. Price walked into oncoming traffic. Witnesses had watched him for several moments and it seemed intentional. "ARE YOU SAYING MY SON TRIED TO KILL HIS SELF? THAT'S BULLSHIT. That bitch right there did this to him!" Bertha continued to scream while pointing at Cameron. Her daughter tried to calm her down but it was very hard. She was so out of control that they threatened to put her out of the hospital several times.

The doctor then told them that even though Malcolm should be OK physically, his mental state was off and he needed to be sent for psychiatric evaluation, but his wife would have to sign for him. This pissed Bertha off even more so that she began cursing Cameron out telling her that she better not send her son away. "He can come home where he belongs. If you send him off you will regret it and that's not a threat, it's a promise," Bertha said to Cameron meaning every single word. Cameron stood there speechless. She didn't know what to say and she couldn't share her thoughts out loud. She was in a fucked up situation. After listening to his last voicemail she knew what had happened. The fool had really tried to kill his self. Malcolm had made comments about not wanting to live without her before but she never took him serious. *What in the hell have I gotten myself into,* Cameron thought to herself for millionth time.

While everyone was meeting with the doctors, Malcolm was in his own little world lying in the hospital bed. He laid there smiling about what he had done knowing that this would make Cameron allow him to come home. His pain meds were starting to kick in and he began to drift back to his childhood. *The eight year old little boy was awakened from his sleep and had no idea what that feeling was under his sheets. He pushed the covers back and saw his mom's best friends mouth wrapped around his private parts. He tried to wiggle and get away but the grip she had on him was too strong for him to do anything. The more he tried to fight, the more violent she became. She had to be totally wasted because she started biting his little dick while she fought to keep him still. Tears streamed down his face and he just laid there and silently succumbed to her torture. He hated the feeling that she was giving him.*

Every night for a whole month straight poor little Malcolm was subjected to the torture he was being given by someone he considered to be his aunt. After one Friday night torture session Malcolm decided he had taken all that he was going to take. His mom was gone out of town and his so called aunt was supposed to be there to check on him and his sister but it turned into what it had been for the past month. When she finished her business, she told Malcolm that the next day she was going to show him how to fuck. Malcolm was terrified.

As soon as she left, Malcolm went into his mother's bathroom and looked into her medicine cabinet. He grabbed a bottle of pills and poured them into his hands then stared at them. There were only about five pills, but he figured if he took them surely they would put his tiny frame out of his misery. Malcolm threw the pills down his throat and washed them down with some water from the sink. He began to get a crazy feeling and even thought he was dying so he went and lay down in his mother's bed. He assumed that his predator was gone but she found him in the bed shortly after he had lain down and tried to pull his pants down. Malcolm found some strength that he never knew he had. He was beginning to feel like a super hero. He kicked her drunk ass as hard as he could and it caused her to stumble and fall. She had went and drank more liquor and was now totally wasted. Malcolm started to think about all the torture she had been giving him and wanted to get even. He reached under the mattress where he knew his mom kept her pistol and grabbed it. He turned the safety off and pointed it at her. She asked *him what was he doing and told him that she was only trying to*

make him feel good and be a man. Malcolm ignored her as thoughts

whirled through his little mind. It wasn't until she charged at him

that he pulled the trigger. He shot her right in the stomach and she

cried out in pain calling him a black ugly little fucker and anything

else she could think of. The more names she called him, the angrier

and hyper Malcolm became. He stood over her and fired another

shot hitting her right above the other blow.

Malcolm's sister ran into their mom's room crying and screaming.

She screamed louder when she realized what was going on. She ran

over and took the gun from Malcolm. He just stood there in a daze.

He was still standing there in the very same spot when the police and

paramedics came.

His "aunt" didn't die but he really wished he would have put bullet

through her skull after listening to the lies she told she told once she

was stable and questioned about what had happened. Malcolm had

to go through counseling and was back and forth to youth court

about the incident. The judge recommended he be sent to a long term

institution but his mom was totally against the idea saying that

nothing was wrong with her son. He was sent off to a facility even after his mom paid money and tried to fight it. Malcolm hated his life. He had to figure out a way to get out of the place he was in. After watching others, he learned to master the art of lying to his therapist and knew how to make everyone think he had taken the medicine he had been prescribed. It was final, when he turned ten he was able to come back home. His mom was able to visit him often and Malcolm had forgiven her for leaving her friend with them. His mom convinced him that she had no idea what had been going on that she would always do everything in her power to protect him from that day on. They packed up and moved down south after that incident and never spoke of it again. His mom found a way to make it look like he had been in regular school the whole time.

Malcolm woke up in a panic but calmed down after he realized where he was. After that traumatic experience from his childhood, he was never the same and to this day he never wanted head from a woman and he would never tell them why. He catered to his mom's needs because she kept her word and protected him from everything since that horrible incident. She didn't even want him to marry Cameron but he somewhat stood his ground and married her anyway. Malcolm was screwed up more than anyone knew.

Chapter 12

Cameron's parents, along with Toya and Shay had made it to the hospital just as the meeting ended. Cameron broke down crying into her mother's arms. Her emotions were all over the place. At one minute she was blaming herself for being too hard on Malcolm, and the next she was ready to curse him out and kill him herself. She wasn't ready to see him yet but she knew she had to face him soon. His mom had gone up to his room and there was no telling what all she had said to him. Cameron's dad hugged her next and told her that he was so sorry for all that she had been going through. He also told her that Malcolm really needed her now and there is no telling what he might do if she turned her back on him completely. It agitated Cameron that her dad was thinking about Malcolm more than her at that moment, but deep down she had those exact same thoughts. Would she be able to live with herself if he really did kill himself? *I need to raise the insurance policy and kill his ass myself because they won't pay for suicide,* Cameron thought to herself. Things were getting crazier by the minute.

When her parents walked away to go to the vending machine, the four girls were left by themselves. "Why you didn't tell us

Malcolm's ass was suicidal? The nigga really walked out into traffic?" Shay said.

"His whole damn family is crazy!! It starts with his damn mama," Toya added.

"I just can't believe any of this. I feel so sorry for you Cam," Sonya said.

"If he would try to kill his self, you know damn well he will kill you. Girl you gonna have to play this smart," Toya said. Cameron reached into her purse and popped three pills without water or anything.

"Are you tryna kill yourself too? What kinda pills you taking?" Toya asked. Cameron ignored her. She didn't even want to get into that at the moment.

"When are you going up to see him?" Shay asked. Cameron finally found her voice and said she was trying to wait until his mom left.

"Umm, judging by the way she's been acting, I really don't think she's going anywhere anytime soon so you might have to suck it up and go on up," Sonya said.

"Is this my fault?' Cameron asked.

"You just married a damn fool," Shay said.

The four of them talked for a little while longer. They were all trying to comfort Cameron as best as they could to help her cope with the situation. After about thirty more minutes they finally made Cameron go on up to Malcolm's room. They all told her they would talk to her later and wished Malcolm a speedy recovery. Neither of the girls wanted to see Malcolm or witness anymore drama so they decided to go ahead and leave. They told Cameron that they would check on her later but made her promise to call them if she needed them no matter what time it was. She agreed and they left.

When she walked into the room the first thing he said was, "Heeyyy baby, I'm so happy to see you. I knew you loved me and would come to take me home."

This fool REALLY is crazy, Cameron thought to herself. She didn't want to set him off in any kind of way so she said hi and asked him how he was feeling. "I'm just ready to go home. The doctor said with pain medication, I should be able to heal at home. I might only be off work for about three weeks," Malcolm said. Cameron felt like she had died on the inside. She started hyperventilating. *Three weeks at home. Everyday. Oh my God!! How in the hell is this gonna work,* she thought to herself. *FUUCCCKKKK,* she screamed in her head.

Malcolm was released from the hospital on Friday evening, the day before Cameron's birthday. She was hoping they would have kept him for a couple more days so she could celebrate in peace, but now she had to come up with a plan to get out. She reluctantly allowed Malcolm to come home. If it had not been for the doctor recommending he be taken to a familiar setting since she wasn't sending him to a facility for psychiatric treatment, and him begging in front of the staff to come home she would have sent him right back home with his mother where both women wanted him.

They made it home before it got dark. Cameron's mom had cooked and cleaned so that Cameron wouldn't have to do too much. She really appreciated her for that. Malcolm was acting like a big baby and acting as if he didn't do this shit on purpose but they all knew the truth. Cameron was finding it hard to play nice when this situation could have been avoided.

As soon as they got settled in there was a knock at the door. Cameron opened the door and found Bertha standing there with pots and pans. "We have food already," Cameron said with an attitude.

She just didn't like this woman and she knew the feeling was mutual. "I just thought I would bring my baby his favorite meal. I didn't mean any harm and I don't want to keep fussing with you. I just want to make sure my son is OK. He asked me to be nice and I think we should try to get along," Bertha said. Cameron felt like this was all a bunch of bullshit, but she instantly thought that if she made peace with her she would be able to get out of the house a little easier. Cameron stepped to the side allowing Bertha to enter. She faked a smile and said that sounds good to me.

Since Bertha had made herself at home, Cameron decided to go take a shower and leave those two alone. She heard Bertha ask Malcolm if he got the results from the DNA test yet and he responded with a simple "No". She fought the urge to go in there and cuss them both out. She was about to get the fuck away from there so she decided to let it slide. She went into the bathroom and turned on the shower then called Keith. They had been texting everyday but she was unable to talk like she wanted to while being at the hospital by Malcolm's side for three days. She told him that she needed to see him soon. "Can you get out in a few?" He asked.

"Yeah, his mom is here and I can tell them I'm running to Wal-Mart. Where is she?" Cameron asked.

"She went out of town to a hair show. I'll be here, just let yourself in," Keith said. Cameron hopped in the shower smiling, thinking about Keith being inside of her soon.

After she finished her shower and dried off, she looked for something quick and comfortable to slip on. She couldn't put on anything that would cause Malcolm to act a fool before she could even get out of the house so she settled for some pink joggers, one of Keith's sweatshirts, and a pair of Ugg boots. *It looks like I'm just going to the store and not to screw my man,* she thought to herself while looking in the mirror. She knew she wouldn't be able to stay longer than an hour but that was more than enough time to get her fix.

She made it out of the house easier than she imagined. Malcolm did ask a few questions and she already had her answers rehearsed. She even had her lie together just in case she didn't make it back as soon as planned. She sent Toya a text to let her know what was up. Toya only replied SMH!! Malcolm wouldn't be able to text because his replacement phone wouldn't be ready until Monday and if he called she would just say she had left her phone in the car which wouldn't be a lie.

Cameron made it to Keith's house in record time and let herself in. She needed him so bad. When she walked in she found Keith in the kitchen cooking him something to eat. He was just getting started but he had it smelling good. Cameron pulled her shoes off at the door, went in gave him a sweet kiss and said, "Let me do that for you bae."

He slapped her on the ass and said, "You know you can't cook, but go ahead and don't burn my food." She playfully rolled her eyes and stuck out her tongue and took over frying the chicken for him. Keith disappeared into the back for a few minutes then came back naked. He eased up behind Cameron and started kissing her neck and fondling her breasts. She let out a soft moan and told him that he was gonna make her burn the food. "Fuck the food, I want you," he said as he pulled his sweatshirt that she had on over her head. "I love this sweatshirt," he said as he unsnapped her bra, turned her around. He then picked her up and sat her on top of the counter. He kissed her passionately and then pulled her joggers off. "No panties, damn you were ready huh?" Keith asked playfully. She arched her back as he entered her and wrapped her arms around him. This was just what they both needed. She leaned forward and thrust her pelvis into him while sucking on his neck. "Shit, you bout to make me cum already girl," he said. He picked her up from the counter and took her into the living room and laid her on the couch never missing a stroke. She cried out in pleasure as he continued to pound her. She dug her fingernails into his back and bit his neck leaving passion marks on him. He was too into her to even care what she was doing. "Oh shit!!" Keith said as they both climaxed. As soon as Keith was about to get up they heard the smoke detector going off and they both laughed. "Fuck the food," she said.

Cameron had drifted off to sleep in Keith's arms and didn't realize it until she was awakened by his phone ringing. She jumped up and asked him what time it was. "It's 10:43," he told her.

"Oh my God! I've been gone almost three hours," she said in a panicked voice.

"I don't want you to leave. I'm tired of this back and forth shit. It's time for you to leave that nigga. We both can't be bae," Keith said.

"I can't leave him right now, not with everything that just happened," Cameron said sadly. Keith had been talking about her leaving Malcolm a lot lately. "I promise, when the timing is right, I'll leave. You know you my bae tho, don't even play," Cameron said.

"You call that nigga bae too so don't even trip," Keith snapped.

"You call her the same thang but I don't even wanna argue with you," Cameron said to him before she kissed him. "Right now, I've gotta get going because I know he's been blowing my phone up. I love you bae," she said before she left.

Just as Cameron suspected, Malcolm had been blowing her phone up. He had called eighteen times. Eighteen got damn missed calls all from home. Cameron texted Toya and told her she was heading home.

"You really tryna die huh?" was Toya's reply. Cameron didn't even text her back. When Cameron made it home she was glad that Bertha was gone. She didn't want to argue with mother and son tonight. She was prepared to deal with the son but not both.

As soon as she walked in Malcolm was on the couch sitting up.

"Why aren't you in bed lying down?" Cameron asked sweetly.

"What did you get from Wal-Mart?" Malcolm asked.

"I didn't realize I had left the bag in Toya's car until I was halfway home. I parked at her house and rode with her. I sent her a text asking her to get it out the car," Cameron lied with ease. "Come and sit with me," Malcolm said. The wheels in Cameron's head were spinning. She was prepared for a screaming match, but Malcolm was too calm and now she didn't know what to expect. She went and sat beside him cautiously. "I'm tired of fighting with you, I know we've both made mistakes, but I want to put it behind us. I can't live my life without you and you won't live yours without me either. 'Til death do us part," Malcolm said and leaned over planting a kiss on her forehead. Cameron was speechless and numb but she was thinking about how that was one of the lines she had skipped in her vows so she was wondering why he always recited it. She was so numb that she didn't even notice that Malcolm was pulling her shirt off until it was too late. She had to think of a way to distract him. "You need to heal before you try to have sex," she tried to plead with him to no avail. He sloppily kissed her and pulled her pants down. *When did he get undressed?* She thought to herself. Before she could protest any further, he was done. *That can't possibly count as screwing two men in the same day,* she thought.

Chapter 13

Malcolm was bored out of his mind and today had only made a week since the "accident". Sitting at home was getting the best of him. He tried to convince Cameron to still take the trip to the mountains for her birthday but she flat out told him no. He knew that she was cheating on him but he had no solid proof. She was taking care of him, and playing nice but he knew it was all just a front. He admitted deep down in his conscience that he had started this, but he would never acknowledge it to Cameron or anyone else for that matter. His mom told him to leave Cameron everyday because one of her coworkers previously informing her about Cameron's boyfriend. She had also informed him that Cameron's boyfriend even brings her lunch to her job. As he sat there, he decided that he would try to catch her in the act. It was time for him to get some proof. He hadn't been out of the house in a week now and it was about time to make a move. He was feeling pretty good with the pain meds so he figured he would be fine.

Malcolm ate a bowl of cereal, showered, threw on some black jeans, a black hoodie, then got in his car and left. He had a little time to spare so he decided he would wash his Mustang since the sun was shining. He loved to wash his vehicles no matter how hot or cold it was so there was no way he could let a sunny day pass him by. While he was vacuuming, he noticed a woman staring at him. She had taken her white Honda Civic through the drive through car wash and now looked like she was just passing time. She looked familiar but he couldn't quite place her. Malcolm being the kind of guy he was, he stared right back at the girl. He finally broke the stare and went to throw something in the trash can. By the time he made it back, she had walked over and was leaning on his car smiling. She greeted him with a hello and Malcolm smiled back. He then noticed that she was the girl who worked at the electric company.

 "I've been waiting on the chance catch you alone so when I saw your car I had to stop. Let me see your phone," she passively demanded. Malcolm was stunned at her straight forwardness and handed her his phone almost immediately. She called her cell phone from his and saved her number in his phone as Callie. "You know, I wouldn't have you out here looking crazy like that wife of yours. You seem like such an awesome guy," Callie said. Malcolm was mesmerized by this blonde haired beauty and decided to keep quiet for a moment. "I could show you a real good time if you let me," she continued. Malcolm finally broke his silence by smiling and letting her know that he was always down to have a good time. They chatted for a few moments before Malcolm realized that he needed to get going. He told her that he would be in touch. When he got in his car, he erased her name out of his phone and programmed her number into his mind. He remembered numbers easily so there was no need for her name to be in his phone. He made up his mind right then that he was gonna finally screw a white girl. He got in his car and drove away grinning from ear to ear.

Malcolm made it to Cameron's job and noticed that she was parked in the perfect spot where he could hide; her car was right in front of a bush. He thought about hiding in the back seat of her car but didn't have the spare key with him so the bush would have to do. It was big so he would be able to hide easily. He drove around and parked on the other side of the building then walked back around and stooped behind his selected hide out. He would never know that when he circled the building to park, he had just missed Keith getting out of her car and leaving.

Malcolm had been hiding in the bushes for about five minutes before he finally heard Cameron's car door open and close. He assumed it was Cameron's mystery man so he jumped up, ran around to the front of the car, and jumped on the hood. Feeling accomplished he screamed, "GOTCHA!!!!" He knew for a matter of fact that he had caught her. The look on Cameron and her coworker's faces were priceless. Cameron was pissed the fuck off and her coworker was scared for her life, not knowing whether to stay put or make a run for it. She didn't have her mace or anything so she was scared shitless. She was only bringing a release form to Cameron that she needed to take with her to the hospital. The only reason she had gotten in the car was because she had a few minutes to spare. Neither of them was expecting Inspector Gadget to jump out of the bushes and onto the hood of the car. Cameron was truly pissed and embarrassed because everyone at work was going to know that she was married to a got damn jackass.

Chapter 14

Cameron was so over Malcolm. That stunt that he pulled on her at work yesterday was too much for her to handle. She wanted to strangle his ass and was seriously considering leaving him, but wondered if Keith was really serious about leaving Phebe. Cameron had been getting nasty text messages on her phone for the last week and knew that it couldn't be anybody but Phebe. She knew that she had to do something because on yesterday if Malcolm would have made it only two to three minutes earlier than he did, he would've caught Keith in her car. He had brought her lunch and she had fed him; fed him right on the back seat as she sat on his face. She never imagined that her life would turn out the way that it had been going. *If I could just turn back the hands of time,* she thought to herself. The girls were supposed to meet up for drinks after work. Cameron had sent out a mass

text because she felt stressed and needed to vent. The day was moving along pretty swiftly and Cameron was ready to clock out. Word had spread about the incident that took place in the parking lot yesterday and she was beyond embarrassed. Malcolm couldn't lie his way out of it either. He had attempted to say he was just trying to surprise her, but how in the hell do you justify hiding in some bushes and then jumping onto the hood of a car screaming "gotcha" as a surprise? It couldn't be justified in her eyes.

Cameron's boss had called her in to speak with her and asked if she needed some time off from work. She could use some time off, but there was no way she could relax while Malcolm was at home since she could barely stand the sight of him. She was also told that the company couldn't tolerate those kinds of behaviors on their property. Cameron told her boss that she understood and promised to get everything under control. She had no idea how to do that but she sure as hell was going to try. She loved her job and wasn't going to allow Malcolm to make her lose it. The only reason she still had her job was because everyone loved her and she was a very hard worker. She was blessed with a wonderful boss and coworkers so she would do everything in her power to get this situation under control.

Malcolm had been calling and texting her all day, but she ignored him completely. She was still pissed at him and he knew it. *He might as well just leave me the fuck alone,* Cameron thought.

The work day was finally coming to an end and Cameron was relieved. She shut her computer down, grabbed her things, and shot out of the door without looking back. Cameron was the first one to arrive at the restaurant so she requested a booth for four. She walked by the bar and a guy complemented her on her outfit. She was wearing a black Marc Jacobs knee length dress with suede black and maroon wedges. Of course she thanked him and kept walking. When she sat down she already knew what she wanted, but she looked over the menu anyway. She wanted a grilled chicken quesadilla with meat and cheese only. Shay arrived next. She was wearing a pretty yellow blouse with some skinny jeans and heels. "What's up Cam?" She asked. "What ain't up," Cameron replied. The waitress came by and took their drink orders, and Shay told her to bring waters for the other two ladies because they should be arriving soon.

Toya and Sonya walked in as the waitress was placing the drinks on the table. After everyone was seated, the women started making small talk. "What did you end up doing for your birthday last weekend since everything happened with Malcolm and we couldn't do anything?" Shay asked Cameron. "Girl, absolutely nothing except pop some pills and slept the day away. I wasn't able to get out of the house because I left the night before to go to Wal-Mart and ended up being gone for almost four hours. Malcolm wouldn't let me breathe in peace so I just went to bed and left him and Kingston up," Cameron said.

"It took you four hours to go to Wal-Mart?" Sonya asked.

"Well, he thought I went to Wal-Mart, but I snuck and went to Keith's house," Cameron answered.

"With me right?" Toya said while taking a sip of water and cutting her eyes at Cameron. Cameron filled them in on everything that had been going on; from Malcolm's wanna be inspector gadget ass, to Keith wanting her to leave Malcolm, to Phebe's constant threats. Shay was the one asking all of the questions today. "Lord, what are you gonna do? I figured Keith would get tired of hiding. Malcolm ass is coo coo for cocoa puffs. Are Keith and Phebe still getting married? What are you gonna do?" Shay said all in one breath. Cameron really didn't know what to do. She felt as if her life was spinning out of control and had no clue how to fix it. She told them she didn't know what to do so she probably wasn't gonna do anything. "Malcolm started this," she said again.

"I told you, I can't judge you because I'm not perfect myself. Love is a hell of a drug, but I'm not tryna get killed behind your drama.

You know Malcolm ass will come looking for me when anything goes down because he's gonna feel like I was in on it. You're gonna have to make some decisions sooner or later, preferably sooner. What would you do if Malcolm was cheating on you?" Toya said.

"I really wouldn't care at all. I wish he would just leave and we can go our separate ways," Cameron said while rolling her eyes.

"You better start being extra careful because not only is Malcolm watching you, Phebe is too," Sonya said.

"On another note, don't y'all forget about my birthday in a few weeks. If y'all bringing anyone just let me know the day before so I can give the restaurant an accurate count," Toya said. Cameron's phone rang and we all knew it was Malcolm by the ringtone. She ignored it. A few seconds later, she received a text from Malcolm stating there was something was wrong with Kingston. Cameron told them what the message said and hopped up gathering her things in a hurry. "Go ahead, I'll take care of your check," Toya said.

"Let us know how Kingston is," Shay told her as she was walking off.

"Girl, ain't nothing wrong with Kingston. I bet money he's just trying to get her home," Toya said.

"He wouldn't do that would he?" Sonya asked.

"Nothing that fool does surprises me," Toya said. The three of them talked a little more while finishing up their meals and headed home.

Chapter 15

Cameron was worried sick on the way home. What could be wrong with her baby? The question as to why Malcolm hadn't called from the emergency room never popped into her mind. She sped home and hopped out of the car without grabbing her purse or anything. She ran into the house and before she could get a word out she saw Kingston laughing and playing on the floor. When he spotted her, he ran to her and jumped into her arms while still laughing. "What's wrong with him?" Cameron asked confused.

"He just wanted to see you," Malcolm replied smiling.

"Are you fucking serious?" Cameron asked.

"Oooh mommy said fucking," Kingston said. Cameron ignored him and walked up to Malcolm. "What kinda games are you playing? What the hell is wrong with you?" She asked. Malcolm ignored her and continued smiling like he was the happiest man in the world wearing a white apron and a stupid looking chef hat. "I cooked dinner, let's sit down and eat as a family," he said.

"I'm not hungry. I was actually eating with my girls before you called and interrupted with your childish ass games," she replied.

"Sit down PLEASE." Malcolm said with a little force. *This motherfucker might be tryna poison me,* Cameron thought to herself. She noticed a strange look in his eyes and tried her best to remain calm while trying to figure out how to get out of this shit. And by shit she meant everything. She sat down at the table and put Kingston in the chair beside her. Malcolm fixed their plates and when he got back up to get the drinks, she switched his plate with hers. *Just in case,* she thought. Malcolm asked about her day as if everything was perfectly fine. Cameron was fuming on the inside. Even though she had switched plates, she still only played over the food. "You can eat. I wouldn't poison you to kill you, I would shoot you in the stomach then shoot myself," Malcolm said.

"WHAT?" Cameron screamed. Kingston looked up puzzled.

"I'm just playing, eat up," Malcolm said. She knew right then and there that he would kill her. She had to figure out a way to end this madness.

Cameron called into work sick the next day. She hated to miss work, especially on a Friday because it would only make the beginning of the next week very hectic, but her head was pounding. She had taken some medication to put her to sleep and figured she must have taken too much. More pills were taken than her normal dosage while Malcolm was in the shower because she hoped to be asleep before he finished. She didn't see anything wrong with it until now. It worked, but now she couldn't move. Her head was pounding and she felt nauseous.

Malcolm got Kingston ready for school and had dropped him off but hadn't returned home yet. Cameron wondered when he was going back to work because he sure seemed fine to her. As soon as she got up and put her feet on the floor, a wave of nausea hit her and she ran for the bathroom. She made it just in time to empty everything she had eaten the day before in the toilet. *Did this nigga try to poison me for real?* When she got ready to wash her face and brush her teeth it hit her that she hadn't taken a birth control pill in a few weeks. *Oh my God, I can't be pregnant,* she thought to herself. She did a mental calculation and realized that her cycle was about two weeks late. *It's probably just stress,* she thought to herself. She was having sex with Keith way more than she was with Malcolm, but she honestly didn't have a clue as to who the father would be if she really was pregnant. Just as she was finishing up in the bathroom Malcolm ran into the house waving a piece of paper and screaming, "KINGSTON IS MY

SON!! KINGSTON IS MY SON!!" Cameron just stared at him with hate in her eyes as she thought about the embarrassment he had caused her the day of that DNA test. How he conveniently called and said he would be late the day before all that drama. She was silently relieved at the results because she could let Keith know to drop his suspicions since he had been talking more and more about Kingston being his son. She was also about to make Malcolm pay big time for making her have to go through this.

On the outside she couldn't help it; her anger erupted like a roaring lion. She went into a rage, yelling, fussing, screaming, and crying about how he made her feel on that day. She picked up a shoe and threw it, hitting him in the head. They argued and argued until Cameron finally pulled away when she heard her cell phone ringing. She grabbed it and looked at the caller ID and noticed that it was her neighbor calling. "Hello," she answered. "Girl, how about Malcolm was downtown not long ago telling everyone he saw that Kingston was his son and showed them the results on a paper he had," her neighbor said. Cameron glared at Malcolm with so much hate. He must have sensed it because he went back outside, hopped in his car and left. Cameron was furious at the news her neighbor had just given her and tried to end the call by saying that she had something she needed to take care of. Her neighbor told her to be sure to call her back because she had something else she wanted to tell her. Curiosity got the best of Cameron so she asked her what was up. Her neighbor began to tell that her that people around town had been talking about the black car that is sometimes parked in her yard. Cameron lied and said that was her cousin's car and she really needed to go but she would call back later. She didn't want to get into that conversation so she ended the call and threw her phone back on the bed, then fell back onto the bed herself. *What kinda life is this?* She thought to herself.

Cameron's phone rang again and she smiled when her brother's picture popped up because he didn't get to call often. It had been about a month since she last talked to him so she was anxious to hear his voice. "Heeyyy brother," she sang into the phone.

"What's up lil sis?" He said.

"Everything, but how are you? It feels so good to hear your voice," she said with excitement, her mood changing instantly.

"I'll be better when I see you, come open the front door," he told her.

"Huh?" She asked as she got off the bed thinking there was no way he could be outside. She opened the front door and threw her phone on the couch when she saw her brother. Running into his arms, she gave him the biggest hug that her body would allow "Oh my God what are you doing here?" She asked while starting to cry.

Tears of joy streamed down her face. She was beyond elated to see her brother and didn't even notice Keith standing behind him. When she finally noticed Keith, he smiled and winked at her. Even though Fred and Keith use to hang out back in the day, Fred would flip if he would've known that his homeboy was sleeping with his baby sister. "I hope you don't mind me bringing Keith by, we got a run to make in a few but I wanted to see you first. I know mom and dad are at work so I'm gonna surprise them later. Why aren't you at work yourself?" Fred asked.

"It's fine. Oh and I wasn't feeling too well this morning but I'm so happy to see you," Cameron managed to say while silently praying that Malcolm would stay gone while they were there visiting. The last thing she needed was for her Malcolm and Keith to be in the same place.

They all went into the house and Cameron asked if they wanted something to eat, hoping they would say no. She really wanted to spend some time with her brother but she had a feeling that Malcolm would be back soon. Keith spoke up first and said he was starving. Cameron cut her eyes at him wondering what the hell he was up to. He just smirked at her. She reached into the cabinet and took out pots and pans and ingredients to make some eggs, sausage, toast, and grits. She figured that should be pretty quick and they could eat and leave in a hurry.

 While they were eating and talking, Cameron froze when she heard a car pull up outside. "Oh shit," Cameron said under her breath but Fred heard her.

"What's going on? You having problems with this nigga or something? We only eating breakfast and talking," Fred said while standing up.

"We have a lot going on but I'll fill you in later. I just wasn't expecting him to return so soon. Sit back down and relax please," Cameron said to Fred then she glanced at Keith who seemed to be amused. "WHOSE CAR IS THAT OUTSIDE?" Malcolm yelled as he walked through the door. "Why you yelling? Let me find out this how you talk to my baby sister on the regular," Fred said while getting back up.

"Oh what's up Fred? When you get here?" Malcolm asked while giving him dap.

"Just got in. This my partner Keith. Keith, this the chump that married my baby sister while I was gone," Fred said.

"What's up partner?" Malcolm said to Keith.

Keith said, "What's up? You have a lovely house and a lovely wife; she just whipped us up some breakfast real quick without exchanging words." Cameron was about to piss on herself. "I'll be right back you guys," Cameron said. As soon as she made it to the hall, she heard Keith asking where is the bathroom. *I know this nigga ain't bout to...* before she finished her thought; Keith was behind her grabbing her ass. "What are you doing? Are you tryna get us both killed?' She whispered through gritted teeth. Keith kissed her and she tried to fight him off but it was no use, her body was like a magnet to his. She couldn't resist him no matter how hard she tried. He knew it too. They could hear Malcolm and Fred still talking in the distance but they were both too caught up in each other to gather their senses at the moment. Keith pushed her into Kingston's room and closed and locked the door. "We can't do this right now," Cameron whispered but Keith wasn't paying her any attention. He bent her over and pulled her dress up, pushed her pink lace panties to the side and entered her in one motion. "Hot and ready like always," he said as he pumped in and out. Cameron knew that they both would be dead if they got caught so she knew she had to take control to end this quickly. She bent all the way over and touched the floor and worked her ass while grinding into him, trying to make him cum. She knew that he wouldn't be able to last long in this position so she kept her rhythm and sure enough he came shortly after. "Get to the bathroom across the hall, NOW!" Cameron whispered to Keith. She opened the door slowly; making sure the coast was clear and pushed him out. Once he was in the bathroom, she made her way to the master bathroom and closed and locked the door. *What in the hell did I just do?* She asked herself as she looked at her reflection in the mirror. She couldn't help but to smile a little. The sneakiness made it so exhilarating. After she cleaned up a little she made her way back to the front and Keith was just sitting back down at the table. "For a minute there I was beginning to think that ol Keith here was back there with my wife," Malcolm said and laughed it off. Fred looked back and forth at Cameron and Keith and knew the deal. He decided it would be best if they went ahead and left after looking at the two of them. "Come on Keith, let's bounce. I'll holla at you later lil sis," Fred said while kissing her on the cheek. "I'm gonna kick y'all asses," he whispered in her ear while hugging her. Cameron didn't even respond to him. She just kissed him on the cheek.

Chapter 16

Cameron made it through the weekend and was glad it was over. They took Kingston to Chucky Cheese on Saturday and he had a ball so that took the edge off things a little. Actually, Malcolm seemed to enjoy himself more than Kingston which made Cameron wonder if she had one or two kids. She decided she definitely had two instead of one. Watching the two of them carrying on made her wonder what Malcolm's childhood was like. The one time she asked he shut her down quickly with a one word answer "fine". Monday morning at work wasn't as hectic as she had anticipated. As busy as Sonya was, she still had helped Cameron out tremendously. Cameron would have to thank her later. Since the day was going so smooth, she was able to leave for lunch thirty minutes early to get to an appointment she had scheduled as soon as she had made it to work earlier that morning. She grabbed her things and left.

Cameron pulled into the parking lot of the Department of Human Services in her Camaro at 11:28. She pulled her three carat wedding ring off and put in the ash tray, took her wallet out of her Coach bag, and walked inside. She was glad she was dressed down in black slacks and a cute top she had gotten from a local boutique. She didn't want to look too out of place. Cameron got the clip board from the receptionist and filled out the application, turning back in within five minutes. She took a seat then waited to be called to the back.

Once she heard her name being called she got up and made her way to the back. The case worker was asking all kinds of questions and she had to lie about over half of them. *I don't know how I'm gonna keep up with these lies,* she thought to herself. She told them that she and Malcolm were separated and he was not helping her financially care for their son. The caseworker asked how long they had been separated and Cameron told him almost a year. She was asked why it took so long for her to request child support and trying to remain thorough with her act, Cameron started crying, stating that she was embarrassed to even be there. The case worker apologized but she also had to ask if there had ever been a paternity test done on the child or if she would need one now. She said that most men deny paternity when you put them on child support and it delays the case. Cameron cried harder while telling the case worker the story about how paternity was established. Her tears stopped the case worker from asking many more questions. She gave them all of the necessary information to Malcolm's job, his social security number, the post office box he uses, and even a copy of a check stub. She was well prepared. Everything went as planned and she would be receiving child support payments within a month, including back time payments. *He gon learn not to fuck with me,* Cameron smiled and said to herself as she shook the case workers hand and left.

Cameron was heading back to work as her cell phone started ringing. The call connected to blue tooth automatically before she could see who it was. She reluctantly said hello and it was her neighbor again.

"What happened to you calling me back?" Her neighbor asked.

"Girl I got busy and forgot," Cameron said.

"Well, I thought you would like to know that your husband is always at the car wash with Callie, you know the white girl that works at the electric company? I just saw them together myself all hugged up skinning and grinning," the neighbor said.

"Is that right?" Cameron said more to herself than to the caller.

"Yep, I just wanted you to know because I would want someone to let me know these types of things," she said while smacking on some kind of potato chip.

"Well thank you for that information, I'll be sure to check into it and let you know," Cameron said.

"Yeah be sure you let me know honey," her neighbor said while still smacking loudly. Cameron disconnected the call and thought about how much she used to underestimate Malcolm. Toya use to always tell her that Malcolm wasn't as dumb as she was thinking. She always said he was crazy as hell, but not dumb as Cameron thought because she didn't give him credit for anything. She was starting to believe that Toya was right.

Cameron grabbed her something to eat from Panda Express and made it back to work with enough time to eat her food in the car before going back inside. As she sat there, she downloaded an app on her phone that would allow her to text Malcolm from an anonymous number. She also made a mental note to check the detailed billing for his phone line later. On her way back she had decided that she was going to see just how dumb he really was. She struck up a conversation with him and he replied instantly:

Anonymous: Hey, what's up?

Malcolm: Who is this?

Anonymous: I'm scared to say right now, but I've been wanting to get to know you better for a long time.

Malcolm: You can get to know me. Just tell me who you are.

Cameron decided that she would say one of her cousin's names thinking there was no way would he keep talking once she said that.

Anonymous: This is Ashley. I know me and Cameron are related but we not close and she doesn't deserve you anyway.

Malcolm: It's been a long time since I saw you. Where you been hiding?

This motherfucker, she said to herself.

Anonymous: I don't live in town anymore, but I'm coming through today. You wanna meet up with me so we can talk face to face?

This asshole better say no, Cameron said…*but if he doesn't, I'll give him a time when I get off and I'll actually have time to see if he shows up.*

Malcolm: Yeah I can meet you

Anonymous: (smiley face) Meet at the park, up top at 6:15

Malcolm: Okay

Anonymous: See you soon

Malcolm: Bet

Cameron was livid. "If this nigga gonna meet up with my cousin ain't no telling what he'll do. Me and Ashley ain't close but she's still family," she said as she gathered her stuff to head back into work. *He better not show up,* she thought.

When Cameron got caught up on the case she was working on, she sent a screen shot of the text messages between Malcolm and "Ashley" to her girls.

Toya: What is this?

Cameron: I downloaded a messenger app and texted Malcolm pretending to be my cousin and look what this motherfucker said.

Shay: OMG!! Malcolm is dumb!!

Sonya: WOW! Really Malcolm…SMH

Shay: You think he really gonna show up? Please say no.

Cameron: I hope not but I don't know what he will and won't do anymore

Toya: Well you said you wouldn't care if he was cheating (confused face)

Cameron: (mad face) Not with my cousin though, and I didn't tell y'all that I heard he's been talking to a white girl? I'm gonna check the phone bill later.

Shay: Lord Lord Lord

Sonya: Y'all got too much going on

Toya: Well for your sanity, let's hope he doesn't show up today because you ain't fooling me with that tough girl, I don't care act

Cameron: I guess only time will tell

Toya: You and your two "baes" gonna be on the big screen one day! LOL

Cameron: Not funny heifer

Cameron was extremely nervous the remainder of the work day because she didn't know what to expect of Malcolm, or how she would handle the unfolding events. She left work a little before five and had some time to spare before heading to the park, so she decided she would stop by J.C. Penny's to browse and hurry the time along. She had done a lot of her Christmas shopping for Kingston online already, but it wouldn't hurt to look for other things as well she thought.

She picked up about four outfits and checked out. When she made it back to her car she checked her phone for the time and it rang. It was Malcolm asking her where she was. She told him that she had to work a little late today but would be home as soon as she finished up. He let her know that it was fine and that he and Kingston were cooking dinner. *He's gonna show up, he's being too nice,* she said to herself when she hung up.

She still had a little time to spare but decided to head on so that she could park where Malcolm wouldn't be able to see her car. When she looked in the rearview mirror a car was blocking her. "What the hell?" Cameron said out loud. It looked as if the car was intentionally blocking her in. "Who the fuck is this?" Cameron said becoming irritated. The door opened to the car and Cameron noticed that it was Phebe. "Damn, not today," she said. Cameron got out before Phebe could knock on her window or anything. Phebe stared her up and down like she was a piece of shit before saying anything. "Look, I know what's going on between you and MY man. Don't you have a husband? What kinda woman are you?" Phebe said. "What are you talking about?" Cameron said.

"Listen, don't try to play dumb or act like I'm a fool. I just came to tell you face to face, woman to woman to stay away from my man," Phebe said.

"Don't you think you need to tell your man to stay away from me?" Cameron said while rolling her eyes. "Whoop her ass Phebe," some loud mouth chick yelled from the car. "I have but you the bitch with the husband… so YOU stay away from MY MAN!!" Phebe said and walked closer into Cameron's space. "Listen you bitch, if you gotta come in MY face about YOUR man then something is wrong with you. Yeah I'm married and you wanna be but he won't marry your ass will he?" Cameron said but was unable to finish her sentence because Phebe pushed her. Cameron stumbled backwards but after she caught her balance she charged towards Phebe. The girl that was with her got out of the car and rushed Phebe to the car because she had saw a cop heading their way. Before she could leave, Cameron threw a bottle at her that had been lying on the ground. Hitting Phebe in the head. "This ain't over bitch," Phebe said as her friend pulled her back to the car.

A few people had taken notice to what had just transpired. Cameron had so much more to say but Phebe was gone just as fast as she had appeared. Cameron got back in her car and couldn't call Keith fast enough. He answered and wasn't shocked at all. He told Cameron that he should've warned her that Phebe had threatened to confront her, but he didn't think they would cross paths so soon. Cameron was pissed. She listened to him apologize the entire ride to her next destination. She ended the call once she parked in the stake out spot at 6:02. "I hope I didn't miss him coming in," she said to herself. No sooner than she got the words out of her mouth, she heard Malcolm's car before she saw it and sighed.

After he drove by and went up to the top, she got out so she could walk closer and get a better look. She wanted to be able to take some pictures too. Her phone beeped with a text message.

Malcolm: I'm here

Anonymous: OK, I'm on my way

Malcolm: Okay

She watched as Malcolm walked around with Kingston, while checking his phone every other second. Cameron decided to head on home so she could beat him. She deleted the app and didn't even bother texting him again. Once again she had underestimated Malcolm. She truly didn't know what he was capable of these days.

Malcolm made it home about an hour later and was shocked that Cameron had beaten him home. "Where you been?" She asked. "Oh we just went to Wal-Mart," Malcolm answered. Cameron just stared at him in disbelief for about three minutes straight. "I saw Ashley earlier," she finally said breaking the silence. Malcolm choked on the juice he was drinking. "Who is Ashley babe?" He asked. Cameron wanted to slap the fuck out of him but instead left him standing there looking stupid.

Chapter 17

The last couple of days had been fairly quiet, Cameron thought as she was sitting at work on Thursday. It was so hard not to confront Malcolm and cuss him out about the Ashley bullshit, but Toya had encouraged her to just wait it out. *You have drama daily, so just wait this out please,* she had suggested to Cameron. Cameron reluctantly agreed. Just by her mentioning Ashley's name had Malcolm acting different. He was being extra nice and had told Cameron that he would be going back to work after Thanksgiving since he was feeling better. *One more week. Lord let me make it one more week until he leaves,* she silently prayed after he told her.

Cameron had put on her best role in order to act sad about him leaving, but quickly flipped it when he started talking about finding work close to home again. "There aren't any jobs around here, but remember you can't quit without having one lined up," she told him. She hated how he always fussed about his job when it was time to go back. He had been off work for three weeks and hadn't put in one application, but all of a sudden wanted a new job when it was time to go back to work. *We wouldn't make it if he was here every day anyway,* she thought to herself.

Since Cameron's boss was leaving for a conference today, he told her that she only had to work until lunch time and she could be off for the whole day tomorrow. Cameron was ecstatic. She wanted to go straight to Keith but decided that she would go on home at lunch time today to clean up and relax, then she could be with Keith all day tomorrow. She smiled just thinking about it. Malcolm would still call and text but it would be easier for her to lie if he thought she was at work.

Lunch time came fast and Cameron wasted no time gathering her things. She peeked in to say goodbye to Sonya before leaving. Sonya had papers all over her desk and was busy working but stood to greet her anyways. Cameron told her she looked nice in her white knee length wrap dress and black and white Steve Madden pumps. "I wish I could wear heels like y'all." Cameron said. "You can girl. Ain't nothing to it." Sonya replied. Cameron reached into her bag and grabbed a gift card that she had purchased for Sonya for helping her out when she had called in. She had failed to give it to her before now with everything that had been going on in her life. "You didn't have to do this, it really was no problem. I just try to help out when I can," Sonya told her.

"I really appreciated it, it's the least I could do," Cameron said.

"So how have you been?" Sonya asked.

"Girl, I'm OK, just taking it day by day," Cameron said.

"Have you ever thought about just being with Keith? It seems like you two love each other, but being with other people is going to cause a lot of more problems on down the line," Sonya said carefully.

"I have, but it's just not as simple as it may seem. I'm gonna get it together soon," Cameron told her.

"OK, I'm not gonna hold you up since you're off, but I just don't want to see anyone get hurt," Sonya said.

"Thank you, I'll be fine," Cameron tried to assure her, even though she had no idea what was bound to happen herself. They gave each other a hug and Cameron left.

Cameron grabbed something to eat from Chick-fil-A and headed on home. She didn't bother calling Malcolm. She figured he would probably be calling her at any minute anyway. She was praying he wasn't home so that she could just crawl into bed. Her first thought had been to clean up but she was exhausted.

When she made it into town she noticed Malcolm's Mustang at the carwash, along with a white girl leaning on his car looking very comfortable. "This must be the Callie bitch," Cameron said out loud. She whipped into the carwash and Malcolm's eyes got so big you would've thought he saw a ghost. Callie ran and jumped into her car and sped off. Cameron hopped out of her car and started screaming at Malcolm. "IF YOU WANT A WHITE BITCH, YOU CAN HAVE HER!! I'M SICK OF YOUR SHIT! I READ THE TEXT MESSAGES BETWEEN THE TWO OF YOU! I EVEN KNOW ABOUT YOU TEXTING ASHLEY YOU DUMB MOTHERFUCKER!! YOU TRY TO BLAME ME FOR EVERYTHING BUT YOU ARE THE GRIMIEST MOTHERFUCKER AROUND HERE!! YOU DON'T EVEN WANT ME...YOU JUST DON'T WANNA SEE ME WITH ANYBODY ELSE!" Cameron screamed.

She kicked his car and when he ran up on her she pushed and slapped him. Malcolm backed away since they were in a public setting, but she noticed that his fists were balled up and jaws were clenched. She hadn't read any messages but he didn't have to know that. Malcolm stuttered and acted like he didn't know what she was talking about. "I'M SICK OF YOU AND YOUR LIES!! JUST GO BE WITH ONE OF YOUR HOES," she continued screaming. "IF Y'ALL MOTHERFUCKERS THINK Y'ALL GONNA HAVE ME LOOKING STUPID Y'ALL DUMB AS FUCK!! I'M SICK OF ALL THIS BULLSHIT!!" She yelled while getting back into her car.

Cameron sped off and headed towards the electric company. She figured Callie was on her lunch break and had to go back to work so she was going to catch her before she clocked back in. She sent Toya a text on her way:

Cameron: My debit card will be under my seat if you have to bail me outta jail and the pin number is 5684

Toya: What the hell are you talking about guh?

Cameron: I'll explain it all later but Malcolm and his white bitch tryna play me like I'm stupid. I just caught their asses all hugged up and shit

Toya: Don't do anything stupid Cam!! You have a job and a son to think about.

Toya: I thought you didn't care if he cheated though…..

Cameron ignored Toya's last text as she pulled into the parking lot of the electric company. She could see Callie still sitting in her car so she pulled up behind her to block her in just in case she tried to leave. Cameron hopped out of her car and headed to open Callie's door. "I guess y'all motherfuckers think y'all gon play me in the same damn town huh? Y'all some got damn fools if you think I'm gonna sit back and be made a fool of. If you want his black ass you can have him but you not bout to play me you white bitch," Cameron said while opening Callie's door. Callie didn't have time to lock the door before Cameron snatched it open. She grabbed her hair and pulled her out the car like she was a rag doll. Callie screamed and while trying to explain that she knew nothing about what was going on. Cameron grabbed Callie by the throat and started choking her. Malcolm pulled up about thirty seconds later while Cameron was still in her rage. Neither one of them knew that Callie had already called the police until they saw the car pull up right after Malcolm was able to separate Cameron from Callie. "So you taking up for this white bitch now?" Cameron said to him. The officer stepped out and asked what was going on. Malcolm was pleading with his eyes to Callie for her to defuse the situation while Cameron wasn't looking.

He gave her some type of signal that neither the officer nor Cameron saw. "Everything is fine officer, we just had a misunderstanding, but we came to a solution right before you pulled up," Callie said while coughing and rubbing her throat. The officer didn't seem too satisfied with her response, but he told them all to go their separate ways. He stood there until they all made their exits. Callie headed back into work while Cameron and Malcolm got into their cars and went separate ways.

Chapter 18

After Cameron left the madness with Malcolm and Barbie wannabe yesterday, she went home, packed a bag, and left. She knew that while Malcolm was in town she didn't have to worry about Kingston so that made her escape that much easier. She didn't give a damn about what he thought. Malcolm truly didn't know who he was fucking with. Cameron could be a cold hearted bitch and he had pushed her to her limits. Cameron had sent Toya a text and told her that she was spending the night with her then she shut her phone completely off. Toya was smart enough to figure out that she was with Keith knowing she didn't give a fuck about what Malcolm would think.

She had no regrets waking up in Keith's arms. She was exactly where she wanted and needed to be. Keith was her distraction away from the real world but didn't realize that she was his too. She didn't know what she would do without him and never really wanted to think about it. They both seemed to always welcome each other with open arms no matter what had been done or said between them. Cameron loved and appreciated him for that.

Cameron was so glad that Phebe was out of town working because she didn't even call before she went to Keith's house. He wasn't home but she let herself in and sent him a text message. When he made it home she cried in his arms until she couldn't cry anymore. She had so much frustration built up and he allowed her to cry it all out. He comforted her and was very attentive to her in every way. He didn't say a word, but only listened. He couldn't bear to give her the news that Phebe was demanding a wedding and she had set a date for next year. She had too much going on already and he didn't want to break her heart anymore. He would tell her at another time, but not right now. He just couldn't bring himself to form the words. He was tired of the back and forth but he just couldn't let go of her. They made love all night. He gave her everything he knew she needed and she didn't know it, but he needed it just as bad if not more than she did. She had been down for him when he didn't have anything and he would always love her for that. He knew that there aren't too many chicks that will stay with a man when he has nothing. In the meantime however, Fred had drilled him about sleeping with his baby sister. There was no need to even lie to him because he wouldn't have believed it anyway so he just told the truth. Fred told him he would kick his ass if he hurt his sister but he also told him to be careful because she was married to a fool. Keith told Fred he wasn't worried about that fuck nigga because he could handle himself.

Keith was still sleeping when Cameron woke up so she decided to get up and cook for him to feed him breakfast in bed. It was the least she could do after he made her feel so good the night before. She smiled and started getting wet as she thought about how he caressed her body from head to toe. She was able to whip up some pancakes, sausage, eggs, and orange juice with what he had in the kitchen. She smiled from ear to ear when she saw the strawberries and fruit dip. *Who says you can't have dessert after breakfast?* She thought to herself.

When she walked back into the bedroom Keith was just beginning to stir a little bit. Cameron sat down with the tray and told him she was about to feed him. He was grinning from ear to ear. He tried to make her eat a little but her appetite wasn't for food, it was for him. When he was done eating, she reached over and grabbed the strawberries and fruit dip. She fed him a couple of strawberries then pushed him back down onto the bed. Sensually, she spread some of the fruit dip on his chest and licked it off like it was candy. Most people used whip cream but she loved fruit dip. She wasted no time making a trail down south where he was fully erect and waiting for her. This was all the breakfast she wanted and needed.

She put a nice amount of fruit dip and his rock hard dick and went to work. She had his toes curling and he was making sounds that she had never heard him make before. "Stop babe, I don't wanna cum yet," Keith mumbled as his eyes rolled to the back of his head. Cameron paid him no attention because she had other plans. When he couldn't hold out any longer, he tried to pull away but she held him tight and sucked and swallowed every last drop of him. *Damn babe,* he said. Keith was in awe. Cameron had visualized this moment in her head for quite some time now and today was the perfect moment to fulfill this fantasy. "Girl, you gon have a nigga head fucked up more than it already is," Keith told her, still unable to move. "Anything for my bae," she said to him.

"Don't think it's over yet," Keith said as he got up and flipped Cameron onto her back. He didn't waste any time diving into her pussy. He sucked and bit her clit so good that she came instantly. He came up for a brief second and grabbed some of the fruit dip. He put a little on her clit and sucked and bit it some more. Cameron grabbed his head and pushed him deeper. She tried to push his head back when she couldn't take anymore but he wouldn't stop. He just pulled her closer and continued devouring her. When he was done feasting, he was fully erect again and ready to fuck the hell out of her. He slid inside of her and went as deep as he could go on the first stroke. Cameron screamed out in pleasure and pain. She grabbed a pillow and covered her face. He continued stroking her and he pulled the pillow off her face and demanded that she look at him. He grabbed one of her legs and pushed it up to the headboard. She grabbed him around his waist and pulled him deeper into her. She was enjoying the fact that she could take all of him like a pro. "Damn bae you feel so good," Cameron said before she started sucking on his neck. "I'm bout to cum," he said.

"Me too, oh shit!!" Cameron said and climaxed with him. Cameron played house with Keith all day until he had to go and make a run about three-thirty that evening. They showered together and got dressed. They almost didn't make it out of the shower because they couldn't get enough of each other.

Keith walked her outside and they hugged and kissed each other until his phone rang breaking the silence. He told her he didn't want to let her go but he really needed to head on out. She told him she understood and dreadfully got in her car after kissing him again. Cameron had turned her phone completely off, but she still decided to leave it in the car. She knew she would have several text messages and probably a few voicemails but she was not expecting twenty-five voicemails or sixty-three text messages. She clicked on Toya's name first since she had texted her and hadn't bothered to wait for her reply before turning her phone off.

Toya:

7:05 pm: Malcolm has been calling my phone but I haven't answered. What happened with you guys now?

7:47: I'm pretty sure you're Keith. I hope y'all got some kinda plan together

8:26 pm: He's texting me now. What you want me to say?

8:48 pm: HELLO

9:52 pm: CAMERON YOUR HUSBAND HAS CALLED MY PHONE SIXTEEN DAMN TIMES AND HE HAS TEXTED MORE THAN THAT

10:59 pm: I'm going to bed!! I hope you know what the hell you're doing

7:13 am: MALCOLM JUST LEFT MY HOUSE!! I THOUGHT THAT NIGGA WAS BOUT TO KILL ME. I TOLD HIM YOU HAD LEFT ABOUT TEN MINUTES AGO

7:45 am: I'm headed to work. I sure hope your night was worth what you're gonna face whenever you decide to show your face. Be safe!!

7:45 BYE

7:46: Crazy ass!!!

There were a couple text messages from her mom asking where she was and if she was alright and all of the rest were from Malcolm. Cameron just shook her head and sighed. She put her car in reverse and dreadfully headed home. Keith called because she was still sitting in the driveway after he left. She told him she was just checking her millions of voice and text messages but she had left a couple of minutes ago. There was no need to call Malcolm so she didn't. Cameron headed home like it was a normal work day. She called Toya but she didn't answer so she sent her a text and said told her that she was heading home.

When she pulled up Malcolm was sitting outside dressed in all black. Cameron began thinking about his ass jumping out of the bushes in all black. "Here we go again," she said to herself. She didn't even have time to get out of the car before he made his way to her door. She tried to get out, but he pushed her back in and told her to crawl over to the passenger seat. She slapped him as hard as she could and he pushed her again and opened his jacket to display the gun that he had recently purchased. *When the fuck did this psycho get a gun and who let him get one?* She instantly crawled over and positioned herself in the passenger seat after seeing the gun. "I don't want to hurt you, but I will if I have to. I only want to talk to you, for right now," Malcolm told her as he got into the driver seat and started backing out of the driveway. He had gone and purchased a gun a few hours ago but it wasn't loaded yet. She wouldn't find out that the bullets were in his jacket pocket until later.

Malcolm drove in silence for the first hour of the ride. Complete silence…for one whole hour. Cameron was scared shitless. She had turned her phone on silent and texted her mom and Toya letting them know that she was somewhere on the Natchez Trace and Malcolm had a gun. She was scared for her life. She told them that she was scared to talk in front of him and that's why she was texting. "I really did love you," Malcolm finally said breaking his silence. Cameron's eyes almost popped out of her head when it registered that he said "did". "All I wanted was a woman who would stay at home and have a house full of babies for me. You didn't even have to work. I went to your job today and they told me you had the day off. I guess you was laid up with that nigga all night because I didn't see your car at Toya's house. She said you had left but I know she was lying. Your car wasn't there last night either. You think I'm so stupid, but I'm far from stupid. When I use to text you on my way home it wasn't because I was being stupid. I was just giving you time to get yourself together so I wouldn't have to kill you. I know you don't wanna be with me but you're mine. We are a family. I MADE Kingston be my son no matter what!! I made it happen because I really don't want to kill you. I told you that I'm not gonna live without you and you damn sho not gonna live with some other nigga. I meant every word I said. Til death do us part sweetheart. I found the birth control pills you been taking so I guess you really won't ever get pregnant again huh? Telling me you will have my baby when it happens. You tried to make it not happen. You WILL have more children because I threw those damn pills away and I dare you to get some more. It's time for you to start acting like a wife. I hate hoes. Do you want me to hate you?"

Cameron remained quiet as he continued to talk and drive deeper and deeper into the woods. She had no idea where they were because he had turned off on a back road from the Natchez Trace. She knew her life was about to end so she closed her eyes and said a short silent prayer to God. *Dear God, I'm really not ready to die so I'm asking you to get me out of this mess. I know I'm not perfect but I try. Please forgive for all the wrong I have done. Please keep my baby safe and away from this fool if he kills me. Amen.*

"Open your eyes up. I've been hearing the talk about some married nigga that's supposed to be your boyfriend. You want another nigga? I've learned exactly where to shoot a person to kill them now. The next person I shoot won't live to tell it. You think if someone screamed out here anybody would hear them?" He asked while facing her for the first time. "How long you think it will take for your little punk ass boyfriend to come looking for you?" She was about to text Keith but Malcolm reached over and grabbed her phone. The screen was locked so she didn't fight him or take any chances to make him any crazier. "Can't NOBODY save you! LOOK AT ME WHEN I'M TALKING TO YOU!!" He screamed while reaching over and turning her head towards his. Cameron really didn't know what to say or do. She knew she really didn't want him anymore, especially after this, but she also didn't want to die so she was once again going to have to swallow her pride. "Do you love me?" He asked her.

"Yeah," she replied dryly.

"Are you gonna be a good wife from now on or do I have to kill you?" He asked.

"Are you gonna be a good husband?" She said a little too sarcastically but he had hit a nerve. "I AM GOOD!!!" he screamed. Malcolm pulled over to the side of the road and broke down crying. *I need to have this fool admitted; Hell I should have had him admitted when the doctor recommended it instead of listening to his bitch ass mama.* Cameron wanted to say it out loud but held her peace so she could at least live a little while longer. "Let's just get married again and start over," he continued to cry. "I'm so sorry; I didn't even put the bullets in this gun. I don't want to kill you. I'm sorry. I just love you so much and don't want to lose you. Please don't leave me. I'll get some help. I'll start back taking my medicine." Cameron was furious but relieved that the gun wasn't loaded. She thought that she was really about to die but she wasn't out of the woods just yet. She wondered what the hell kind of medicine he was talking about and who had he shot before? *I hate this crazy ass motherfucker,* Cameron thought. She decided to play nice, get out of this situation, and do everything in her power not to be put in it again. She didn't know what other choice she had. Telling him she hated him at that very moment would most likely cause more trouble than it would be worth. "We can start over. Let's just go home," she said while rolling her eyes as he cried in her lap. "Do you love me?" He asked. Cameron bit her lip and gritted her teeth and eventually mumbled yeah. "Say it," he said.

"I love you," Cameron said dryly. *I wish I could load the gun and kill his ass and leave him out here for the wild animals to have a feast. Stupid bastard,* Cameron thought to herself.

Chapter 19

Monday morning at work Cameron was thinking about how she had been walking on egg shells over the weekend. She only had a three day work week ahead and then she would be off two days for Thanksgiving, then hopefully Malcolm would really be leaving going back to work. She figured if she played the "good wife" role like he wanted, and did everything in her power to keep the peace everything would be good. She only talked to Malcolm when he talked to her. He was walking around acting as if he hadn't threatened her life on Friday.

All day Saturday he tried to get her out of the house. He asked her if she wanted to go out to eat, to the movies, even shopping but she wouldn't budge. She just wanted him to disappear…like really dis-a-fucking-pear. Forever. He even tried to make her feel guilty about not going to church on Sunday, but she just stared at him like the crazy fool he was. He wouldn't go to church and take the chance of leaving her alone. To seal it all, Kingston had called them both some crazy fools on Sunday. He was repeating more and more of the things he heard day by day.

Cameron sat in the house all day Saturday and Sunday feeling depressed. Phebe was at home with Keith for the weekend, and even though she couldn't get to him that made her angry and jealous. In a perfect world she would be married to Keith with two kids and they would live happily ever after, but she wasn't living in a perfect world. Nowhere near perfect. She was living in hell, pure hell on earth.

When she was looking for her car keys earlier that morning Malcolm smiled and held them up in front of her to see. He told her that he would drop her off at work and pick her up. He even said that he would bring her lunch. Cameron retaliated for the first time since he had scared the shit out of her. She told him that she was perfectly capable of driving herself to work and didn't need a damn chauffeur. Malcolm simply ignored her and told her to let him know when she was ready. Cameron felt so helpless. *I'm not ready to die so what choice do I have but to do as he says for now?* She thought to herself. She started getting mad all over when she thought about being dropped off at work. *Just a few more days,* she told herself while trying to relax.

While Cameron was finishing up with a case her phone vibrated. She really hated to look at her phone fearing it was Malcolm, but she picked it up anyway. She opened the text and a picture of a newborn baby appeared. She looked at the number and it seemed familiar so she thought for a few seconds before it hit her. Nikki. "Why is this bitch sending me a picture of a newborn baby?" Cameron said while getting angry thinking about this dumb hoe. She was about to reply but another message from Nikki came through saying: Here's a picture of Mackenzie, your step daughter. Cameron was speechless. She remembered hearing a rumor about Nikki being pregnant but she never looked into it to see if there was any truth to it and she NEVER even thought about her being pregnant by Malcolm. *I knew there was a good damn reason for that bitch to call me, and this psycho ass motherfucker wanna blame me for everything when he will fuck anything that walks. At least I only have one person on the side..* Cameron forwarded the picture to Malcolm and said meet your daughter you lying son of a bitch!! Within seconds Malcolm was calling. Cameron got up and closed her office door before answering the phone. "You black bastard!! You doing all this threatening me and you got a baby by that trailer park trash bitch!" Cameron hissed into the phone. She was thankful that she remembered she was at work before answering. "That ain't my baby. She lying, just calm down sweetheart," Malcolm said.

"I don't wanna hear that bullshit and don't call me sweetheart. How about you send a damn DNA truck on wheels to her house like you did me, you lying son a bitch!!" Cameron calmed herself down as Malcolm was babbling. Whether this baby was his or not, this was just the distraction she needed to get him off of her back. She never even had time to confront him about anything that she knew about him because she was trying to save her life; but now she knew that he would happily take his black ass on back to work. She smiled to herself and told Malcolm, "If that bastard baby is yours, you can pack your shit and go move in that house you had to rebuild. Goodbye." *Click.*

Cameron was happy to end the call with the upper hand, but what if the baby really was Malcolm's? What would she do? What would his crazy ass do? She also wondered what he meant that day in the car when he said he made Kingston his son no matter what? Cameron had a million questions and no answers. She didn't even bother replying to Nikki. She was sick of confronting these women over Malcolm's black ass. She knew that she would do something else crazy so she decided she would focus on Malcolm. Since Cameron had no car and Sonya took off the whole week for the holidays, Cameron decided to order in from Bulldog Deli since they didn't charge an arm and a leg for delivery. On her lunch, she started a conversation with her girls. She started the chat by sending the picture Nikki had sent her.

Shay: Whose baby is that?

Toya: Damn you done had a baby in the midst of all your drama?

Cameron: HELL NAW!! Nikki sent this and said it's my step daughter. She said her name is Mackenzie.

Shay: OMG!!

Toya: WTH??

Shay: What did Malcolm say?

Toya: I swear your life needs to be in a book or movie, hell both!!

Sonya: Goodness. This is just too much!

Cameron: I sent him the picture then he called. He said it ain't his baby. Was telling me to calm down and shit

Toya: I guess he'll send a DNA truck to her house next

Cameron: Not funny but I asked him the same thang. He embarrassed the fuck out of me so we will see what he does

Cameron: Sonya I wish you was here. Malcolm dropped me off at work so I'm stuck.

Toya: WTH? Dropped you off... lawd!! I just don't know what to say anymore. How he acting all innocent?

Cameron: EXACTLY

Toya: Y'all both need help!!

Shay: Y'all crazy!!!

Toya: Beyond crazy lol

Sonya: Why did he drop you off? What's that supposed to do? I'm glad I'm not at work but I'll be back next week chile.

Toya: Right, like Keith hasn't been to her job. Malcolm just dumb

Cameron: Toya what time your dinner start next week? Malcolm should be gone and I can come in peace

Toya: 7:30....6:30 for Shay and Sonya

Sonya: I will be on time ma'am

Shay: I will too thank you very much

Toya: Hmph. Only time will tell

Keith called Cameron so she stopped texting the group. *Hey bae,* she said while smiling from ear to ear. He changed her mood instantly. "Hey baby girl, are you out for lunch today?" He said. She sighed and told him about how her morning had gone. She was able to send him a few text messages over the weekend but this was her first time talking to him. She was smiling just to be able to hear his voice because at one point she thought she would never be able to hear it again. "Ima come through and see you," he said.

"As much as I would love that, it might not be a good idea. He's probably out there hiding in the bushes again and we don't need any more drama," Cameron said.

"When you gonna leave that fool? I'm tired of this shit. I'm beginning to think you like living a double life, having two niggas and shit. You getting a thrill outta calling both of us bae," Keith said. Cameron got sad and sighed then told him as soon as she comes up with a plan. She told him she wishes it was as easy as people seem to think it is. She hated having these kinda conversations with Keith. It broke her heart when he made it seem like she enjoyed the position she was in. They talked for the rest of her break and Cameron asked

Keith if he would go with her Toya's birthday dinner next weekend. He agreed without hesitation but before he hung up he told her that Phebe found the thong she left under the pillow. Cameron was speechless. She sure left it under Phebe's pillow as payback for her approaching her in the parking lot that day. There was no need in her lying because Keith would have known she was lying so she didn't say anything at all. "Don't forget you the one with two bae's. Don't pull no mo shit like that. I got out of it so it's all good," Keith said before he hung up.

Cameron's next two work days were very busy. She was determined to complete all of her tasks before the holidays. She hated leaving work over the weekend and leaving any over a holiday was much worse. She spent lunch in the office again because Malcolm really dropped her off all three days. Sick bastard really kept her car keys like she still couldn't do anything if she wanted to. There are ways around everything but she was just playing it safe until he left.

On Wednesday night Malcolm told Cameron that his mom was expecting them at noon the next day for dinner. Malcolm knew that Cameron had plans to eat with her parents, but he felt like since he was leaving the next day he could manipulate her into going to his mom's house first. Cameron froze after he said it and stared at him. She counted to ten before speaking. "I have been walking around here like a prisoner in my own damn house letting you control me like some puppet. I'm not about to keep playing these games with you. You already know that I am eating at my parent's house. I will compromise by coming to your mom's house later for a few minutes, but I am not missing thanksgiving with my parents. Especially with my brother being here and he is leaving tomorrow evening. You might as well cut the shit," Cameron said with a menacing look. Malcolm thought about the picture of the baby. He didn't really know if the little girl was his or not so he decided to back off. He was not going to her parent's house because he didn't know exactly how much she had told them. He really didn't want to face her dad because he felt like he had let him down. "Well Kingston is coming with me," Malcolm said. Cameron wanted to have her baby with her but she wasn't about to start another fight, so she said, "Fine, I'll just take Kingston to my parent's house now to spend some time with his uncle." She knew that Malcolm wouldn't dare come so she quickly grabbed her keys and yelled for Kingston to come on. "Are we going to see Unk?" Kingston asked.

"We sure are baby," Cameron smiled and replied while zipping his jacket. Kingston was ecstatic.

Cameron went to her parent's house and made a short visit of about fifteen minutes then asked to use her mom's car and headed to Unk's house. Fred was out and about anyway so she didn't feel guilty for not staying at her parent's house long. She knew that Malcolm would ride by the house so she wanted her car to be there in plain sight for him to see the entire time. She also knew he would be calling but she would answer a couple of calls anyway. She made it to her destination just as Keith was pulling up. They got out of their cars at the same time and Kingston ran and jumped into Keith's arms. "Hey Unk, where you been? I missed you," Kingston said.

"I been working lil buddy but I missed you too," Keith told him. They headed into the house and Keith asked Cameron how she got out. "I'm at my parent's house. Can't stay too long. I'm sorry about that little mishap. It won't happen again," she said.

"Ol girl should be here in a couple hours," he said while turning on cartoons for Kingston. Cameron tried not to roll her eyes but she wasn't successful. Keith walked up and grabbed her from behind and started playfully biting on her neck. She turned around and started kissing him passionately. Cameron pulled back when she heard a cell phone ringing. It sounded like it was coming from Kingston's jacket. Kingston was glued to the television and didn't hear anything. Cameron picked up his jacket and the ringing got louder. She reached into the pocket and pulled out a cell phone. "Whose phone is this in your jacket pocket Kingston?" She asked.

"Oooh that's my phone daddy gave me. Its ringing, let me see it mommy," Kingston said while jumping up to get the phone. It stopped ringing but started right back. Kingston grabbed the phone and answered. "This dumb ass nigga bought a three year old a cell phone," Cameron said to Keith. "Hey daddy…. I'm watching cartoons with Unk and mommy;" they heard Kingston say to Malcolm.

"Let me speak to daddy Kingston," Cameron said.

"You bought him a cell phone Malcolm, why?" Cameron asked. "He's playing and having a good time. We will be back soon;" she told him and hung up. Malcolm called right back and told her he wasn't done talking. "I'm about to come up there," he told her.

"Come on then. I don't care," she said knowing he wouldn't dare come to her parent's house. He just wanted to see if she would try to stop him but she didn't fall for his lame ass tricks.

After she hung Kingston's phone up while shaking her head, she turned to Keith and ushered him to the bedroom. He picked her up and carried her down the hall while kissing her. She wrapped her arms and legs around him and held on tight. She needed to feel him inside of her so bad. She was about to bust a nut just from his touch. She hopped down once they made it to the bedroom so she could regain control.

She pushed him down into the chair. Fucking was on her mind. They could make love another day. She ripped his shirt off and kissed his chest. She was already hot and wet and he was hard and ready. She pulled his pants off and grabbed his dick and devoured it. She teased his balls with her tongue and made him move trying to get away from her. After licking him like her favorite lollipop, she stood up and slowly sat down on his big hard dick.

After a few slow movements up and down, she began to ride him like the stallion he was. "Ooh bae you feel so damn good, shit!!" She said while riding him and loving every minute of it. She squeezed her pelvic muscles together and rode him until they both climaxed. "Damn I needed that," she said as she fell back onto the floor and closed her eyes. "I'm not done." Keith stood up, flipped her over, and entered her from the back. He knew that Phebe was in route towards home but couldn't resist Cameron. She was his drug that he wanted all the time. He slapped her ass and thrust himself deeper into her. "Whose pussy is this?" He asked.

"It's yours bae," she said as he fucked her harder and deeper.

"Who's the best?" He asked.

"You are without a doubt big daddy," she said.

He flipped her over and pushed her legs up behind her head and went in as deep as he could causing her to cry out in pain and pleasure. "You so damn wet. I'm bout to nut all in this pussy," he told her. She pulled him deeper into her and they both came within the next minute.

Neither of them was able to move for about fifteen minutes after fucking each other's brains out, but they knew they had to get up. Cameron couldn't stand Phebe's bitch ass but she didn't want to get caught there. They finally made their way to bathroom and took hoe baths because time was of the essence. Keith went to the front and played with Kingston for a few minutes before Cameron finally

announced that they better get going. He walked them outside and

told them he would see them soon. He gave Cameron a kiss and

stood there watching them until they were out of sight. Cameron

wasn't ninety seconds up the road before she met Phebe driving in

the opposite direction. She was so glad that she wasn't in her car and

that it was dark. *Damn I left just in time. One of us would've had to*

die if I would have gotten caught there.

Chapter 20

Cameron had a wonderful Thanksgiving dinner with her family. Kingston didn't want to go with Malcolm so she was very happy to have him there with her instead of his crazy ass people. Everyone laughed and talked like the good old days. Charlotte, Cameron's sister even came home for Thanksgiving and brought her husband. Cameron looked at him kinda sideways because he seemed a little feminine to her. Fred picked up on it too and they shared a private laugh about it. Charlotte had moved away as soon as she graduated and this was only her second time coming home. Her parent's begged her to come home more often but she always told them that she couldn't get off work.

Cameron's parent's wanted to talk about Malcolm but they didn't want Fred to know everything that was going on. They knew if he found out it would have set him off, and they didn't want him to get in any trouble while he was at home visiting. His hot temper had simmered down a lot but anything could trigger it, especially someone messing with his family. Informing him of what was going on would be big trouble. He loved both of his sisters but he was always closer to Cameron because he didn't like the way Charlotte treated the baby of the family.

After having such a great time with her family, Cameron had to literally force herself to get up and go to Bertha's house. She really didn't want to go, but needed to keep the peace since Malcolm was leaving the next day. He had already called her about five times but she ignored every one of his calls so she figured it was time to get up and go.

 She kissed her siblings and told them she hoped it wouldn't be too long before she saw them again. Charlotte promised to start coming home more often and told them she was about to leave too. She told them that she needed to make one last stop to see one of her old girlfriends before leaving back out. Cameron asked her who, but Charlotte told her it was nobody she knew and cut the conversation short. Cameron sensed a little shadiness in Charlotte's response but she just shrugged it off and turned to her brother. She cried when she embraced Fred. She missed her brother so much but she knew that he was doing well for himself and had to go back. She longed for the day that he would come back home for good. She wanted to tell him everything that had been going on in her life but she had promised her parent's that she wouldn't. She scooped Kingston up, kissed her parent's, and told them that she would call them later and left.

When Cameron and Kingston made it to Malcolm's mom's house, she noticed all of the people and thought to herself there was no way they even missed her and Kingston. Malcolm walked outside as they were getting out of the car. "Why you didn't answer your phone buddy?" He asked Kingston.

"It was in the car," Cameron answered for Kingston.

"You didn't answer yours either. I guess it was in the car too," Malcolm said to Cameron. She just ignored him. They walked inside and spoke to everyone. Bertha walked up and gave Cameron a fake hug and then picked Kingston up and hugged and kissed him, putting her cheap red lipstick on his cheeks. "Hey granny baby," she said to him.

"Hi granny," Kingston said. He loved both of his grannies because they let him have his way. She asked them if they wanted anything to eat and Cameron declined but Malcolm fixed them both plates anyway. He had life messed up if he thought she was going to eat anything from that woman's house. "Don't act like you too good to eat my cooking," Bertha said while rolling her eyes. "I'm not hungry," Cameron said through gritted teeth.

"Did you roll your eyes at your mother in law?" One of Bertha's sisters asked Cameron. "Look, I'm trying to be nice. I'm not hungry so I would appreciate it if y'all would just shut up and leave me alone!" Cameron snapped.

"Who you telling to shut up, with your trifling ass?" the sister asked. Cameron desperately wanted to cuss out and kick all of their asses, but she also didn't want to do anything to set Malcolm off and keep him from going back to work tomorrow. Cameron got up, grabbed Kingston and headed for the door. She heard Malcolm calling her name but she was not stopping. "You know they just be playing. Come on back in, don't leave," he pleaded with her. Cameron put Kingston in the car and then turned back around to face Malcolm. "You're always making excuses for your crazy ass people. This kinda shit happens every single time I come down here and you never stand up for me, but wonder why I never wanna come. They call me every name they can think of, but do they know that you are the one that has a child by another woman? Do they know that you are the one around here fucking white bitches? I'm sick of this shit and the best thing for me to do is go home. You can stay down here as long as you like but I'm going home," Cameron said while shaking her head and getting into the car.

"Well can you at least let Kingston stay?" Malcolm asked looking pitiful.

"Do you want to stay here with your daddy Kingston?" Cameron asked him.

"Are you going to see Unk? I wanna see Unk again," Kingston said.

"No baby, I'm going home," Cameron replied not even caring that Malcolm would more than likely question Kingston if he stayed. Kingston finally agreed to stay with Malcolm and Cameron drove off.

Cameron left without looking back. On the way home, she decided to stop by the store to pick up a few items. She knew that Malcolm was going to want some sex before he left and she was not in the mood to give him any. Not that she ever really was, but she most definitely wasn't in the mood now. Cameron started drifting back to through her years of the resentful marriage. She thought back to her very first time with Malcolm, which was two days after her wedding since a big argument prevented them from consummating the marriage on their wedding night. When she finally decided to go home two days later, Cameron was excited to see what Malcolm was working with. She just knew that since she waited to have sex with him until they were married she was going to be in for a treat. He had talked so much noise and her expectations were through the roof. She hated to think about Keith and how good he was, but she found herself thinking about him and wondering if Malcolm could be better than him. If he was, she was going to be in heaven for the rest of her life.

Since two days had passed since the wedding she didn't know whether to expect candles, a hot bubble bath, or soft music. She had no clue what her new husband had in store, but she expected romance. She shook off the thoughts of not knowing his real first name to keep her from changing her mind about leaving her parent's house. Malcolm had called again begging her to come home, so she told him she would be there in thirty minutes. She figured that there was no need in staying another night in her childhood room and since it was already dark outside she reluctantly agreed.

When she made it home he was laying on the couch watching the discovery channel. Though a little let down by the scene, she decided to drop it. She made her way down the hall to the master bedroom and was even more disappointed. The bed hadn't even been made. *What the fuck have I gotten myself into?* Cameron dropped her bag on the floor and was about to go turn on the shower when Malcolm walked into the room. *"Baby, I'm sorry about not telling you my real name and I'm sorry for listening to the rumors about you being with another man the day before our wedding. I know you wouldn't do anything like that. You're not that kind of woman. Let's just forget about all that and make a good marriage out of this. I love you,"* Malcolm said. Cameron started to feel a little guilty about being with Keith the night before she got married and even the entire two weeks before, but she would never let him know.

"I'm sorry too," she said.

"Now I wanna get some of this good loving," he said while pushing her down on the bed. Cameron told him that she was just about to take a shower but he said he was ready to have her right then and there. He sloppily kissed her and pulled her clothes off. Malcolm was pumping and yelling that he was about to come before Cameron could even try to get herself in the mood. *No the fuck you not*, she wanted to scream but thought to herself instead.

"Damn that was good baby, I ain't never came that fast, you got some good pussy," Malcolm said to her while getting up from the bed. Cameron just laid there unable to move. She was in shock. *Whoever said to wait to have sex before marriage needs to be executed,* she thought.

"I'll be ready for round two in a few minutes," Malcolm said. That turned out to be a big ass lie. There was no round two; there was not even a round one in Cameron's eyes. He got back in the bed, wrapped his arms around her, and was snoring loudly within minutes. He wasn't small he just didn't know what the hell he was doing and couldn't last long at all. *Lord just rewind to three days ago, PLEASE!! I swear I will just run away!!* Cameron thought. Cameron pulled into Dollar General and saw a few familiar faces. She really didn't want to be bothered with anyone; she just wanted to grab some pads and a few other items then head home. No her period hadn't come on yet, but she was going to put on a pad to keep Malcolm from touching her. She knew that she was wrong but what else could she do? He wasn't going to touch her if her period was on, so she knew she had to really make him believe it. He had caught her in a lie before about being on her period so she would play the game

better this time. She grabbed a few items and was almost able to check out without distractions. Just as she was walking out of the door, in walked the pastor who conducted her and Malcolm's counseling session. "Hello Sister Cameron," he said. Cameron ignored him and he turned around and followed her out the door.

"Can I speak with you for just a minute please," he called after her?

"What do you want? If you're not apologizing for being a fake then I don't want to hear it. Better yet, I don't even want a fake ass apology from you," Cameron snapped at him.

"I'm really sorry for anything you may have thought I said was out of line in the past," he was saying until Cameron cut him off.

"Anything I may have thought? You have got to be kidding me," Cameron said.

"OK, I'm sorry for my actions. I just wanted to check on you and Malcolm. How are things going with you two?" The pastor asked.

"My feelings are the same about you as the day you conducted that fake ass session. I made it perfectly clear that I had nothing else to say to you and it still stands. You and Malcolm grimy asses can have all the sessions you like but leave me out of them. Now if you'll excuse me, I was heading home before I was so rudely interrupted and I would like to get there now," Cameron said.

"If you ever need anything, anything at all please don't hesitate to call," the pastor said. Cameron looked back at him, rolled her eyes, and flipped him the bird then continued to her car.

Shortly after she made it home she decided to group message her girls. They had texted a little earlier but she didn't have her phone on her at the time. She had been ignoring them quite a bit lately but it wasn't intentional. She just had too much shit going on.

Hey ladies, how was y'all Thanksgiving?

Shay: It was fine, I'm so stuffed I can't move.

Toya: Everything went well, we playing board games right now and having so much fun.

Sonya: It was fine, how was yours?

Cameron: Where do I begin? It started out fine. My whole family was here, even my sister. I hate that my brother had to leave today but I enjoyed spending time with my whole family. Things got crazy when I went to Malcolm mama house

Shay: Oh lord, what happened down there?

Sonya: That's sweet that you had both of your siblings home for thanksgiving but do we even wanna know what happened at Bertha's house?

Cameron: I wasn't hungry because I ate at my parent's house but went down there anyway because I promised him that I would come. When I refused to eat, I got called stuck up, trifling and I don't know what else by his mama and aunts.

Sonya: What did Malcolm say?

Cameron: NOT SHIT!!

Toya: Lord, y'all couldn't get along on Thanksgiving...just give up lol

Cameron: And I'm pregnant

Toya: BY WHO?

Shay: OMG

Sonya: Lord hammercy

Cameron: I'm shame to say, but I really don't know who it's by, but the chances of it being by Keith outweigh Malcolm's chances a million to one

Toya: Girl!!!! What are we gonna do with you?

Shay: How far along are you?

Cameron: Probably only about a month or a little over. I really don't know

Sonya: This is some non-stop drama. How did this happen? I mean I know how, but how?

Cameron: I forgot to take my pills

Shay: You need to try the Mirena

Toya: Have you told Keith?

Cameron: Nope, it took a lot to tell y'all

Shay: So what are you gonna do?

Cameron: Honestly I haven't even thought about it. I just bought and took a test when I got home. This shit wasn't supposed to happen. My life is a mess

Toya: Wellll...never mind, I'll hush. You better be smart though. You are dealing with two men who both want kids.

Cameron: I know. Well I'm about to take a shower and try to stay calm so that Malcolm will really leave tomorrow. I'll talk to y'all later.

Cameron ran a hot bubble bath, poured herself a glass of Moscato not even thinking about being pregnant and grabbed her phone to text Keith.

Cameron: Hey bae, what you doing?

Keith: Thinking about you, what you doing?

Cameron: Sitting in the tub, sipping some wine, and thinking about you

Keith: Damn, I wish I could be in that tub with you

Cameron: Me too

Cameron: He leaves tomorrow so I'm chillin tonight, trying to keep the peace

Keith: I'm really ready for you to leave that nigga.

Damn I don't wanna have this conversation right now, Cameron thought.

Cameron: Me too bae, but I can't just up and leave. His crazy ass will kill both of us

Keith: That nigga ain't the only one that got heat

Cameron: We will figure it out. I promise. I love you!

Keith: I love you too

After Cameron finished with her bath and put lotion on, she put one of the pads on that she had just bought from the store and climbed into bed. She didn't realize that she had drifted off to sleep until

Kingston ran and jumped into the bed hugging and kissing her. "I saw Carlie," he said.

"Carlie, who is Carlie," Cameron asked. *I know this motherfucker didn't have my baby around that white Callie bitch,* Cameron thought.

"He talking about Kayla, my cousin," Malcolm said while stuttering. Cameron didn't believe him at all and she let it be known by the look on her face. "Can I sleep with you mommy?" Kingston asked.

"Sure you can baby. I would love that," Cameron replied while kissing him.

"Mommy and daddy want to sleep alone tonight buddy," Malcolm said while winking at Cameron. "I won't be able to fulfill any of your fantasies tonight, I have a visitor," Cameron said to Malcolm as nice as she could. Cameron took Kingston's clothes and shoes off, put on his pajamas and put him next to her in bed. Malcolm hopped in bed between them and Cameron rolled her eyes. After Kingston was asleep Malcolm started rubbing on Cameron. She shifted and told them that her period really was on. He kept rubbing and when he reached between her legs and felt the pad she had on he said damn and turned over and went to sleep. Cameron smirked and

scooted further away from him. *Yes,* Cameron said to herself. She

just didn't know what she could do to make herself want to have sex

with Malcolm.

Chapter 21

One Week Later

Malcolm left a week ago and Cameron was beyond ecstatic. He was still a little salty because he couldn't get any, but Cameron paid him no mind. The few days leading up to his departures were torture, he even told her to let him look and see if her period was really on but she told him to shut the hell up. Then, he started complaining about being away from home once again which made Cameron bite her tongue so hard she drew blood. She just needed him to leave by any means necessary. They finally said their goodbyes and she was free. She wanted to turn some flips when he left but was scared that he would come back if she celebrated too much. Of course he still called constantly but that was better than him being at home in Cameron's eyes. She had just dropped Kingston off with her mom, and was at home getting ready for Toya's birthday dinner. Keith was going to get one of his friends to drop him off and then ride home with Cameron and spend the rest of the weekend with her. She couldn't wait. A whole uninterrupted weekend with him would have her on cloud nine. She was also excited about Toya's dinner because the people she invited were always laid back and the atmosphere was always pleasant.

Cameron decided to go out on a limb and wear some red Jessica Simpson pumps with a black fitted dress by Marc Jacobs. She had just the right accessories to make it pop. Once she was done getting dressed she applied her make-up, including her favorite lip stick which was Ruby Woo. After grabbing her cell phone and purse, she checked herself in her full length mirror one more time and headed for the door. She turned her XM satellite radio station to THE HEAT and sang every song the came on. That station was the shit. She called Keith to make sure that everything was straight on his end and he let her know everything was all good. She thought about texting Toya to let her know that Keith was coming but she decided against it. *Everything should be fine;* she thought to herself and continued having her own little party.

She pulled up to the restaurant about ten minutes ahead of time and spotted several familiar cars. She decided to go on in and when Keith called she would just walk back outside to meet him. Cameron walked in and spoke to everyone who had already made it then struck up a conversation with one of Toya's cousins who had done her hair a couple of times before. The girl was so gifted with her hands that Cameron didn't know why she didn't have her own salon. "Girl you look good. And you're wearing heels! Oh shoot," Toya said to Cameron. "I decided to try something different and step outside the box but please believe I got my flats in my purse. You look great yourself." Cameron replied. "Thanks girl," Toya said. Toya had on a pink blazer with a multi-color mini skirt over tights. She always wore heels so it wasn't a shock that she was rocking some bad black

Christian Louboutins. Everyone was looking cute and feeling good. Shay and Sonya walked in looking fierce. They sat down next to Cameron and began talking about nothing particular. Just as the waitress came to take their drink orders, Keith called Cameron's phone letting her know that he was outside. She excused herself and walked out of the restaurant to meet him. He was thanking his friend for the ride when Cameron walked up and hugged and kissed him. Neither of them saw the car that was slowly coming towards the entrance because the head lights were not on.

They made their way back into the restaurant and as soon as Keith walked in, all eyes were on him. "Well hello Keith Edwards, long time no see," Emily, one of Toya's friends said. Toya noticed the look on Cameron's face and discreetly asked Emily how she knew Keith. She didn't want any drama at her dinner. Emily told her that she knew him from college, he use to talk to her roommate at the time. Toya sent Cameron a text filling her in because there was no telling what all she was thinking. Toya knew Cameron all too well and was well aware that she really wanted to pop off just that fast. She would probably fight over her "bae" Keith before her "bae" Malcolm. She told the girls that it's easier to call them both bae so she doesn't say the wrong name and they all just laughed at her. The dinner went very well with everyone enjoying themselves. They all made plans to meet up at Rick's after the dinner to continue the celebration except the love birds. Cameron and Keith were among the first to leave. Cameron had already told Toya that this was going to be a much needed relaxation weekend with Keith. She was ready to enjoy her man without any distractions. Toya told them that they didn't have to rush but Cameron was ready to get home so she told them all she would catch them later.

Keith told Cameron he would drive so he hopped in the driver seat. He noticed that she needed some gas and fussed at her about letting her gas tank get to E.

They headed towards the closest store when they left the restaurant. After he pumped the gas and went in to pay for it, a car pulled up and almost hit him before he opened the door. "WHAT THE FUCK!" he yelled. He was about to cuss the driver of the car out until Phebe jumped out. He couldn't do anything but drop his head when he saw her. "WHAT THE FUCK ARE YOU DOING WITH THIS BITCH?" Phebe screamed at Keith while pointing to Cameron.

"WHO THE FUCK YOU CALLING A BITCH?" Cameron screamed back while getting out of the car. Keith stood between the two women while they argued back and forth both reaching around Keith trying to throw the first punch. A few people had stopped and were staring. One girl had her phone out and it was obvious that she was recording. Phebe was able to push Cameron and make her stumble then Keith turned to Phebe and pushed her toward the car she got out of. The girl that was with her never got out or said a word. He yelled and told Cameron to get back in the car. She wanted to knock the fuck out of Phebe for pushing her but didn't want to continue making a scene at the store; plus she could tell that Keith was pissed off so she got back in the car. Keith was standing there talking but she couldn't hear what he was telling Phebe.

Within minutes he was getting back into the driver seat of her car. Phebe stood there for a few minutes yelling and cussing them both out, but Keith just drove away. "Damn I guess she followed me up here," Keith said to Cameron after about two minutes of silence. "She's following us now," Cameron said while looking back. "FUCK!!" Keith screamed. "She wasn't supposed to even be here this weekend," he continued. She said this was her weekend to work. Keith's phone started ringing non-stop. When there was finally a break from his ringing phone Cameron's phone started ringing. "Don't answer that phone," Keith told her in a stern voice. Cameron wanted to answer but she didn't want to start an argument with him. They had been riding for about forty-five minutes with Phebe and her friend still trailing them. She kept calling and flashing the lights trying to get him to stop. Cameron thought she was going to run into the back of her car a few times. She would have if Keith would not have sped up. Keith was in Cameron's hometown, but decided it was best not to keep their original plans and go to Cameron's house. He didn't know if Phebe knew where Cameron lived or not and he didn't want to be the one to disclose that information to her. He also didn't want to make a scene and cause her nosey ass neighbors to come outside. It didn't matter if there was drama in the day or night, they would always be there.

He chose to drive another twenty-five minutes to his parent's house and Phebe continued to follow. He couldn't get away from her no matter how hard he tried. He picked up his phone and called his mom and briefly told her what was going on. When they reached his parent's house his mom was already standing outside. He hated to put her in the middle of his madness but he didn't have much a choice at the moment.

Before Keith could get out of the car Phebe had already parked and jumped out of her car. "Stay in the car," Keith told Cameron. She rolled her eyes at sat there. She almost wanted to slap him as bad as she wanted to slap Phebe. Keith and Phebe yelled and screamed at each other. His mom tried to get them to be quiet but of course they didn't listen. It was good they didn't have neighbors right beside them. Cameron heard Phebe telling Keith that she couldn't believe that he would pick a trick ass bitch with a husband over her. She called Cameron all kind of names. His mom kept trying to get them to calm down to no avail. "GET OUT THE CAR YOU STUPID ASS HOE ASS BITCH!" Phebe screamed at Cameron while rushing towards the car. Keith grabbed her and told her to chill the fuck out and don't call Cameron a bitch anymore. "You protecting this married ass skank?" Phebe asked Keith in disbelief.

She broke away from him and rushed towards the car again. This time she was able to open the door. Cameron hopped out and Phebe swung at her, hitting her on the shoulder. Cameron swung back but ended up hitting Keith because he jumped between them. Cameron was able to hit Phebe on her right arm then one time in the face after Keith stumbled and fell. The two women cursed each other out while trying to get the best of each other. Keith's mom had ran in the house to get his dad. Through the screen door, he looked as if he didn't want to get involved in the drama but came out of the house anyway. Keith stumbled again because he couldn't control his women, and Cameron was able to push Phebe down. Keith's dad grabbed Cameron and pulled her back right before she was able to jump down on Phebe.

It seemed like it took forever to finally separate everyone and afterwards Keith started crying, saying he didn't mean for any of this happen. "I'M READY TO GO HOME!" Cameron screamed. "WELL TAKE YO BITCH ASS HOME!" Phebe, screamed back at her. Keith's mom pulled Phebe towards the house and his dad pulled Cameron toward her car. He tried to push her toward the driver seat but Keith hopped in it before she could. Cameron went around and got in the passenger seat and he sped off, leaving Phebe standing in his mother's yard screaming and crying. His dad didn't say a word because he truly felt his son's pain and no one had any idea just how much.

On the way home Keith started talking about Cameron leaving Malcolm and him leaving Phebe again. He accused her of loving that drama shit and having two niggas that she called bae. He had heard her more times than one call Malcolm bae and she always said she was just trying to keep him calm, but he was over those excuses. He told her that he had put everything on the line and it was time for her to make a decision. As she sat quietly listening to him, she decided to text her girls to let them know what had just happened.

Cameron: Y'all ain't gon believe what the fuck just happened!!

Sonya: Oh lord, do we wanna know?

Cameron: Phebe followed Keith tonight and waited until we left the dinner then followed us to the store. We all go into it.

Shay: OMG!! NOOO

Toya: WTH?? What happened after that? I know that didn't end like that

Cameron: She followed us all the way to his mama house. We passed a few licks but I couldn't get her like I wanted to. I wanted to beat the fuck outta her. His mom and dad had to help break everyone apart.

Sonya: Goodness. The drama just never ends huh

Cameron: We headed to my house now

Toya: We? Who is we?

Cameron: Me and Keith

Sonya: What in the hell?!

Shay: What? Where is Phebe?

Cameron: She was standing her bitch ass in his mama yard crying and screaming when we left

Toya: So, you mean to tell me that this girl done followed y'all from town to town, y'all end up at his mama house, fuss and fight, and then he leaves her, his fiancé, standing in his mama yard and is headed home with you???

Cameron: Yep. Now he asking when am I gonna leave Malcolm so he can leave Phebe and we can be together. He talking about I like this drama

Toya: And what's your answer?

Cameron: I don't know. I don't think he is serious

Sonya: I'm starting to think you like this drama too chile

Shay: Lord Lord Lord!! Y'all are crazy!!

Toya: You don't think he's serious, but he left his fiancé standing in his mama yard and is headed home with you? SMH!! Damn you can get two men and I can't get one.

Toya: Phebe gonna fuck y'all up! You better hope she don't get in touch with Malcolm

Cameron: She don't know how to get in touch with him

Shay: Really? These small ass towns

Sonya: I just don't know what to say

Cameron: Everything will be ok. I'll figure it out.

Cameron stopped texting but had no idea how she would figure it out or how anything would play out.

Chapter 22

Cameron sat at her desk feeling extremely stressed at work on Monday morning. She was even looking stressed. She had bags under her eyes and her hair was a mess and on top of that she had no energy to put on any make-up which was out of her character. She had just gotten her hair done a few days ago but it was hard to tell. Her hair was always on point, so anyone who saw her in her current state knew that something was terribly wrong. Knowing that she looked a hot ass mess, she sent her beautician a text to see if she could squeeze her in as soon as possible. She was a loyal customer so it shouldn't be a problem.

The pleasant and relaxing weekend she had envisioned was far from that, in fact it was the complete opposite. The only thing that went according to its plan was Toya's birthday dinner. To make things worse, Phebe was calling and texting both her and Keith's phones nonstop. Cameron even expected her to pop up at her house, but she never did.

After Keith kept whining about her leaving Malcolm, she was mentally drained and ready to go to bed. She was tired of explaining to him that it wasn't as easy as he thought. He had broken up with

Phebe several times before but her clothes never left. They weren't even married and never really broke up but he couldn't see her point of view. For the first time since they had been together, they didn't have sex while spending the night with each other. Neither initiated anything because they were both pissed off at the complicated situation they had created.

The next day Keith finally answered his phone. The first call he answered was from his mom. Cameron could hear his mom defending Phebe so she rolled her eyes and got out of bed. She even heard her asking him why he just wouldn't leave Cameron alone because she was up to no good. She mentioned something about her having some kind of Voo Doo on him. Cameron wanted to grab the phone and cuss her out but that would only cause another argument between her and Keith. She thought they would have some amazing morning sex, but he killed her mood again. While Cameron was in the front watching TV, Keith was still in the back on the phone and her phone starting beeping with text messages:

Phebe: What kinda woman are you?

Phebe: You ain't a woman at all. You a tramp bitch!!

Phebe: Don't you have a husband you could be fucking instead of my man?

Phebe: Yo mama probably a hoe too!!

After that message, Cameron decided to reply:

I could fuck my husband but I love Keith's big dick better, you bitch!!

That message was followed by pictures of Keith sleeping in Cameron's bed, as well as Phebe's bed. She even sent pictures to let her know that she was very familiar with her house. Phebe started calling Cameron's phone instead of texting after she received those pictures and messages, but Cameron turned her phone off and started back watching TV. After about ten minutes, Keith came from the back. "WHAT THE FUCK DID YOU JUST DO?" He yelled at Cameron.

"I did what she wanted me to do," Cameron replied while rolling her eyes. "And you better watch how you talk to me, with your crybaby ass," Cameron said. She mumbled so he couldn't hear the last part. They spent the rest of that day arguing. Still no sex. Cameron was ready for him to go home if they weren't going to have any peace. She didn't have peace with Malcolm and refused to be constantly arguing with two men.

On Sunday morning they were finally talking to each other without arguing and screaming. Cameron decided to get up and go grab some breakfast. She called in an order of pancakes, sausage, and eggs from a local restaurant and went and picked it up.

When she made it back with the breakfast Keith was laying on the couch watching TV. They ate together then he grabbed her and started kissing her. She was instantly turned on and made her way on his lap. She pulled her shirt over her head and he unsnapped her bra then removed it. She held her head back in ecstasy as he kissed and sucked her breasts. She wanted to feel him inside of her so bad that she hopped up and pulled off her pants and panties while he pulled his off at the same time. *Fuck the foreplay,* she thought. She eased back down slowly on his dick and threw her head back. He grabbed her hips and met her thrust for thrust. "Damn I love you bae," she said while continuing to ride him.

"I love you too Phebe, and I'm sorry," he said.

"What the fuck did you just call me?" Cameron said while jumping up. He didn't even realize his mistake until she said something.

"Shit, I'm sorry bae. My mind is so fucked up right now," Keith said. Before he could even finish with his explanation Cameron had all of her clothes back on and was standing there pissed the fuck off. Keith left to go home, and that was the end of their crazy weekend together.

Cameron stopped thinking back to the weekend when her phone rang at her desk. Her boss needed her to send a document to the courthouse that she could've sworn she had sent already. Her personal and work lives were both in shambles. Cameron was happy when five o'clock rolled around. *What a fucking day,* she thought to herself while getting in her car in route to pick up Kingston. After she safely made it home with her son, they relaxed together for the rest of the evening.

Cameron had just put Kingston in bed when she heard her phone beeping with a text message. When she picked it up she noticed that she had several text messages from the group chat, a couple from Malcolm, (along with five missed calls from him), a missed call from her sister, and one from Keith. Her sister had been calling her on the regular since Thanksgiving and they had become closer than ever. Cameron felt good talking to and confiding in her. She had always wanted a closer relationship with her sister so she would be sure to call her back soon. She was glad that Thanksgiving had mended their broken relationship. Cameron still didn't know exactly why it was broken in the first place but she was just thankful to have her sister in her life. She opened up the group chat first:

Shay: I finally got my tree up (sent with a picture)

Toya: Pretty! I'm finishing mine up now. I'll send a picture later

Sonya: That's pretty Shay. We are putting ours up tomorrow.

Toya: I can't believe your slow ass finished first Shay

Shay: Whatever. Where's Cameron. She has been MIA since Friday.

Toya: IDK. I haven't talked to her either. I called a few times but her phone has been going straight to voicemail every time I try. Hopefully everything is OK

Sonya: I hope she's OK with all that drama she had going on this past weekend.

Shay: Me too

Cameron: I'm here and the drama has been nonstop. I turned my phone off because I was tired of Phebe calling so I'm just now getting all of my messages.

Shay: What else happened?

Cameron: Phebe kept calling and texting all weekend while Keith was here

Shay: So he really stayed. Ump ump ump

Cameron: Yep. Then I sent her pictures of us together in his house and mine. Then when we finally had sex, he called me her name and I put him out.

Toya: YOU DID WHAT??

Toya: WHAT DO YOU BE THINKING?

Cameron: I wasn't thinking. I was mad at the moment.

Toya: So what you gonna do if she send those pictures to Malcolm?

Sonya: Wow Cam!! What were you thinking?

Cameron: I didn't even think about her sending them to him. She doesn't have his number though.

Toya: Did you give her your number?

Cameron: No

Toya: MY POINT EXACTLY!!

Sonya: You gotta be smarter than that girl

Shay: Lord Cam!!

Cameron was tired already and didn't feel like being lectured anymore so she opened Keith's messages next.

Keith: First off, let me say I'm really sorry for calling you by her name. My head is just really fucked up. I know I would be pissed if you called me his name but you call us both bae so that won't happen will it? It's like you wanna just keep playing games but I really want you and only you. I done laid it all on the line, but you ain't making no moves so I think it's best if we just chill out for a while. I love you so much, but you don't want me like I like want you so I gotta stop hurting ole girl. I shed tears in front of you and it didn't even faze you. You think a nigga wanna cry for real? I'm lost and confused. Until you figure out what you wanna do, we gotta chill. I'll always love you no matter what.

She didn't even reply to him or look at anymore messages. If she would have checked her other messages she would have known how pissed off Malcolm was. She just went and popped four pills, downed them with some Orchard Splash cranberry juice then went to bed and cried herself to sleep. Keith said he was lost and confused, but how could he not understand that she was too?

Chapter 23

Malcolm was glad to be back working, but he still hated to be away from home. It wasn't that he didn't trust Cameron specifically, he really just didn't trust women period. The experience he went through as a child left him that way, and he always told his self that he would never fully trust a woman. Any woman who drinks could especially not be trusted, and he knew Cameron drank from time to time. She didn't drink before they got married and he never once thought that he led her to do it afterwards. He had also watched his mom and sister play men like keyboards throughout the years so he learned not to trust women through them too. Women had ways of breaking men down and he always said that he would get them before they got him, which is why he was the way he was. All he wanted was for Cameron to quit work, have two or three more children and take care of home like a respectable woman was supposed to do.

Cameron would kill Charlotte if she would have known that she had been giving Malcolm information on her. Malcolm had no idea that stranger that he had confided in at that truck stop about the DNA test he wanted on Kingston was Charlotte's ex-husband who had also recognized Malcolm from Facebook. Charlotte always seemed obsessed with keeping up with her family but never called them or tried to have a decent relationship with them. She was now divorced and for Thanksgiving had brought a friend home pretending to be her husband, making everyone believe that she was still happily married. She had gone to the justice of peace and didn't have a wedding so no one knew what her husband looked like anyway because she didn't invite her family up. She just called her parents one day and told them she was married. They were disappointed that she didn't allow them to share in her happiness but there was nothing they could do about it.

Charlotte's husband was tired of her crazy ways and when she had an abortion behind his back knowing how badly he wanted kids, he divorced her. That marriage only lasted nine months. Her ex-husband had told her about his conversation with Malcolm, not knowing that she would use the information against her sister at a later date.

Malcolm was driving down the road when his phone started beeping with a text message. Before he could pick it up it beeped a couple more times. When he finally grabbed his phone and opened the messages he didn't recognize the number, but he noticed Cameron with a man with a caramel colored skin complexion. He looked familiar but Malcolm couldn't place him and had to pull over to keep from wrecking. He was livid. The pictures were of Cameron and this dude in bed together. They were in HIS bed and some other bed too. He immediately called Cameron's phone back to back to back but she didn't answer so he sent her a couple of text messages. She didn't reply. He called two more times and she still didn't answer. If he stopped his route now, he could make it home by noon the next day and that's exactly what he did after he called his boss and told him that he had a family emergency. He was headed to kill Cameron and the man in the picture if he could find him. He kept trying to figure out where he knew the man from but couldn't wrap his brain around it.

Chapter 24

The next morning Cameron woke up with a banging headache along with being nauseous. She felt like shit. She was barely able to get Kingston ready for school but that was all. She called and asked one of her cousins to come and pick him up and drop him off for her, and then she got back in bed. She called her boss and left a voice message saying that she was sick and couldn't make it in today. This was her second time having to call in and she felt terrible about it, but there was no way she could make it to work with how she currently felt.

She went right back to sleep and woke up at about eleven o'clock feeling somewhat better. She rolled out of bed and her phone beeped with a text message. She picked it up and noticed that she had ten missed calls from Keith and several text messages. "I thought he said it was over," she said while rolling her eyes. She dragged herself in the bathroom. She turned the shower and got in with hopes that the hot water would bring her back to herself and relieve some of the nausea.

As soon as she got out of the shower her phone started ringing again. She knew that it was Keith by the ringtone because she hadn't changed it yet. She wanted to, but couldn't bring herself to do it because she actually missed him. In the midst of her thoughts, she realized that she hadn't heard from or called Malcolm back. *Strange that he hasn't called,* she thought. Just as she was about to check his text messages from last night, Keith started calling back again. "I thought you said we needed to chill out for a while," Cameron said as she answered the phone.

"Look, now is not the time for all that so listen up. I overheard ole girl on the phone with Charlotte. She had it on speaker and it seems like they reconnected or some shit around Thanksgiving. Anyways, your trifling ass sister gave her Malcolm's number and she sent him those pictures last night that you sent her," Keith said. Cameron couldn't move because was in shock. "So I don't know what's gonna become of all this, but Malcolm knows. Has he called you?" Keith asked.

"He texted me and called but I didn't answer or check the messages," Cameron said while finally finding her voice. "You need to be careful bae," Keith said.

"So now I'm your bae again?" Cameron snapped.

"Look, focus and kill the dumb shit. Be safe and keep in touch. I don't have a good feeling about this shit," Keith said. Cameron told him OK and hung up. She glanced at the clock and noticed that it was 11:43. She finally opened Malcolm's text messages from the night before:

Malcolm: ANSWER THE GOTDAMN PHONE!!

Malcolm: I'M GON KILL YO MOTHERFUCKING ASS!!!

Malcolm: AND THAT NIGGA TOO IF I SEE HIM! WHO IS HE?

Cameron's knees went weak. She called Malcolm's phone but he didn't answer. She tried again and he still didn't answer. All of sudden she felt sicker than she had felt earlier. Her phone beeped and she checked it. It was a message from the group chat:

Sonya: Malcolm left from up here about fifteen minutes ago looking for you. I guess he's trying to surprise you but he looked pissed off. What's going on?

Cameron didn't bother replying at the moment. She hurried up and finished slipping on some clothes. She threw on the quickest thing possible which was a pair of skinny jeans that were almost too little and a Hollister tee. Her sneakers were right by the bed so she threw them on without socks. She grabbed her phone, purse and keys and headed for her car. Once she pulled out of the driveway she picked her phone up and texted back:

Cameron: A whole bunch of shit has happened but I don't have time to text it all right now.

Just as she sent that text, she met Malcolm down the street in a curve flying. She sped her car up and panicked even more.

Cameron: He's chasing me. I can't text and drive this fast. Talk to y'all later.

Cameron sped down the highway driving ninety plus miles per hour trying to get away from the lunatic who was chasing behind her. She gripped the steering wheel tight as her heart beat rapidly and tears streamed down her face. She could not believe she had been so stupid and sent those pictures. Not thinking had most definitely backfired on her. One part of her wanted to just let go of the wheel and let her Camaro crash so that this chase would end, however her sane conscience thought about her son Kingston. Not to mention the child she recently found out she was carrying. With that second thought, she quickly cast her impractical thinking aside and regained her composure. The black car behind her was closing in and all she could do was pray. The expectant mother had ignored the beeping

noises until her car began to slow down. She then realized she was

running out of gas, but the crash that came from behind sent her car

flipping violently off of the highway.

Chapter 25

Malcolm had really lost his mind this time. He couldn't believe what he had just done, but at the same time he wished he could have done more. After he ran Cameron off the road, he didn't even stop to check on her. He went to the store and made an anonymous 911 phone call saying that someone had just run off the road and their car had flipped a couple of times. He hung up before the operator could ask if he was still on the scene. Malcolm's car had a few scratches so he decided he would take it and put in the shop to kill time until someone called about Cameron. He got a rental which wasn't out of the norm because he sometimes rented cars for his trips home from work so no should question that. His plan was to act like he was still at work whenever the call came through. *I hope they don't call my boss since I told him I was going home,* he said to himself while trying to figure out a plan.

After he got his story together the phone call came through about Cameron's accident. He told them that he was actually close to home and would be there as soon as he could. He didn't know if her parent's had been called or how she was doing. Mentally, he was a complete mess.

Malcolm finished off the last beer out of the twelve pack he had brought before heading to the hospital two hours later. He almost wrecked a couple of times before he got there because he was so out of it. Cars were blowing at him the entire time. Once he got to the hospital and was told that Cameron was in coma, he went ballistic and started cussing the doctors and nurses while telling them that they better save his wife. He told the doctors that he was not leaving her side no matter what. When he saw her parent's walk in, he went numb. He had no idea how much they knew and when he saw two police officers walking closely behind them he fainted.

When he woke up he was in a room and the same two officers he saw before he passed out were there. "Mr. Price, how are you feeling?" asked the first officer.

"I…I don't know. What happened? Where am I?" Malcolm replied, trying to act as if he was still out of it.

"You fainted when you saw us walking toward you," said the second officer. Malcolm began to fake a hysterical cry as he asked, "WHERE IS SHE?! WHERE IS MY WIFE?! WHAT HAVE Y'ALL DONE TO HER? I NEED MY WIFE!!" The second officer asked Malcolm to calm down several times before he actually did so, but it was obvious that the officer was not falling for Malcolm's bullshit. "We need to ask you a few questions Mr. Price," said the first officer. Malcolm immediately began to become defensive, asking the officer, "You think I had something to do with this? WHERE IS MY WIFE?!"

In reality, Malcolm was afraid of what the officers may already know. He began to become fidgety, and he broke out into a nervous sweat. The second officer said, "Mr. Price, no one is saying that you had anything to do with what happened to your wife, this is just routine protocol," while side eyeing the first officer. Malcolm realized that he needed to calm down and cooperate with the officers to keep the heat off of him. "Go ahead officer, I'm just so stressed out and worried about my wife," said Malcolm.

"Can you tell us what happened to your wife?" asked the first officer. Malcolm immediately flashed back to the pictures that were sent to him of Cameron and some other man in his bed. He was becoming angry just thinking about it. He thought about how he had called and texted her and how she never answered. He began to think that every single time he called and she didn't answer because she must have been with that man from the pictures. He thought about how quickly he made it home and how he met Cameron in the curve down the street from their house. He internally reminisced about how he turned around and chased her driving at least ninety miles per hour down the road. He replayed the scene of him ramming his car into the back of her car, causing her to run off of the road and flip at least two times that he knew of which made him more and more nervous as he began to speak. "All I know is I received a call from someone saying that she was in an accident," said Malcolm. The second officer asked Malcolm, "Where were you when you got the..."

Malcolm answered before the officer could finish his question, "At work, I was at work and I got here as soon as I could. It took me two hours to get here because I wasn't too far away."

"Well you didn't even allow me to finish my question but OK Mr. Price. We will be following up with your boss to confirm your route," the officer said while smirking.

"I... I was actually heading home to surprise my wife and I told my boss I had a family emergency. I get lonely out there on the highway and I was missing my family. I don't want to get fired so I said I had an emergency but I was going right back to work," Malcolm said.

"My my my, didn't that story change up very quickly," said the same officer, not believing a word that Malcolm was saying.

"I just need to get to my wife. I think she ran off the road trying to kill herself," Malcolm said while crying hysterically. Both officers were looking at him in disbelief now. They couldn't charge him off of suspicions so they had no choice but to let him go, however, they advised the medical staff of their suspicions and requested that he be supervised when visiting with his wife.

Cameron's parents didn't know the full story yet, but they knew something was terribly wrong from the moment they received the phone call to come to the hospital right away. When Malcolm passed out after seeing the officers, they knew that he had done something to hurt their baby girl. They weren't allowed in the room while Malcolm was being questioned and Cameron's dad was about to lose his mind. He was feeling guilty about even introducing his baby girl to that bastard. One of his coworkers he considered to be a friend had told him about Malcolm and he was sold from the very beginning. He never did his own research; he just took the word of his friend.

It was hard for Cameron's mom to calm her husband down because she was a nervous wreck herself. She slipped away from him and went to the bathroom to make a call that needed to be made. She knew that Keith would want to know about Cameron, and Cameron would want him to know and she knew how to get the message to him. She had to make it quick so that she could be by her husband's side.

Malcolm was in the back with the officers for about fifteen minutes. Those fifteen minutes seemed like a whole hour. The officers walked out and headed towards the elevator and Malcolm walked out about two minutes later. "WHAT DID YOU DO TO MY DAUGHTER YOU ASSHOLE?" Cameron's dad screamed while charging toward Malcolm. Her mom tried her best to hold him back she was no match to the power he had. Cameron's mom was thankful the officers hadn't gotten on the elevators and heard all of the commotion. They rushed back and grabbed Cameron's dad just as he put his hands around Malcolm's neck. After everything calmed down and the officers separated Malcolm from his father in laws strong grip, they heard a code blue called over the intercom. Everyone panicked and

Malcolm passed out again assuming the code had been called for Cameron.

I hope that you all have enjoyed the crazy ride so far. I hope that you are anxious for part II because it is coming very soon. Will Cameron survive the crash? Will Malcolm get away with trying to take the life of his wife? Will Keith walk away? What about Phebe? Be ready to continue the ride. I would love to have your honest thoughts on the book. Please leave me a review on Amazon or any of my social media sites and I promise I will read them all. You may also reach me via email @ authortwylat@gmail.com or on Facebook, Instagram & Twitter @authortwylat

I look forward to hearing from you guys & get ready for part II!!

COPYRIGHT NOTE

© Copyright November 2015 Twyla T.

PUBLISHER'S NOTE

30621794R00134

Made in the USA
San Bernardino, CA
18 February 2016